BROKEN ARROW

Charles D. Richardson

The setting for this Historic Fiction Novel is during the height of the Cold War. The United States and the Soviet Union each had enough nuclear weapons stockpiled in their vast arsenals to destroy the world several times over. Both sides were in a continuous state of alert mainly because of mistrust and an impending attack. Intercontinental Ballistic Missiles were in the development stage: long-range bombers were the war machines of choice.

It was a tense time of Ground Observer Corps, bomb shelters, practice alerts, Sputnik, Nuclear Winter, and Mutual Assured Destruction. School children hunkered beneath their desks while sirens wailed. Daily Strategic Air Command training flights mimicked an assault on a Russian city or military complex using chaff drops, air refueling, simulated bomb drops, simulated ground missile threats, and maximum fighter attacks. Cat-and-mouse games were practiced with other military commands and with the Soviet Air Defense system at all hours.

This story is an accurate account of a dangerous Strategic Air Command training flight known as a Uniform Simulated Combat Mission, which went terribly awry during an Air Defense Command fighter intercept and resulted in the declaration of a Broken Arrow.

Library of Congress Control Number: 2009929247
ISBN-13: 978-0-9789510-3-0
ISBN-10: 0-9789510-3-4
Printed in La Vergne, TN on acid free paper

INTRODUCTION

The setting for this Historic Fiction novel is during the height of the Cold War. The United States and the Soviet Union each had enough nuclear weapons stockpiled in their vast arsenals to destroy the world several times over. Both sides were in a continuous state of alert mainly because of mistrust and the threat of an impending attack. Intercontinental Ballistic Missiles were in the development stage: long-range bombers were the war machines of choice.

The United States Air Force Strategic Air Command (SAC) and the Air Defense Command (ADC) aircraft were the primary deterrents. Pilots of these aircraft stood by in nearby buildings waiting for the klaxon to blare.

The Soviets had a similar program. It was a nerve-wracking environment. In some scenarios, the pilots didn't know if the alert was real or for practice until hours into the mission.

It was a tense time of Ground Observer Corps, bomb shelters, practice alerts, Sputnik, Nuclear Winter, and Mutual Assured Destruction. School children hunkered beneath their desks while sirens wailed. Daily SAC training flights mimicked an assault on a Russian city or military complex using chaff drops, air refueling, simulated bomb drops, simulated ground missile threats, and maximum fighter attacks. The ADC intercepted incoming unidentified aircraft that had incorrectly penetrated an Air Defense Identification Zone, not knowing whether the aircraft was a Soviet bomber until identified friendly by an ADC pilot. Cat-and-mouse games were practiced with other military commands and with the Soviet Air Defense system at all hours.

This story is an accurate account of a dangerous SAC training flight known as a Uniform Simulated Combat Mission, which went terribly awry during an ADC fighter intercept and resulted in the declaration of a Broken Arrow.

BROKEN ARROW

Military code word for a nuclear weapon accident.

"If we had to bomb Russia, we were on a suicide mission."
— Colonel Howard Richardson (USAF Ret)

"When my brother and I built the first man-carrying machine, we thought that we were introducing into the world an invention which would make further wars practically impossible."
— Orville Wright, 1917

Also by Charles D. Richardson

The Pact
Maxima 120

Coming Soon

Flying Machines

Despite the most elaborate precautions, it is conceivable that technical malfunction or human failure, a misinterpreted incident or unauthorized action, could trigger a nuclear disaster or nuclear war.

Introduction of U.S.-Soviet Treaty U.S. Arms
Control and Disarmament Agency
September 1971

CHAPTER ONE

Air Force Major Howard Richardson opened his eyes and squinted to avoid the ray of Florida sunshine streaming through a slight opening in the venetian blind. He listened to familiar sounds coming from outside his door and smiled. The night before, he had mentioned to his wife, Vivian Ann, that he might sleep until 8AM. Now, his built-in clock and the angle of the sun's rays told him it was near the appointed time. A glance at the clock confirmed his guess—which meant that Vivian had been successful in quietly calming five-year-old Blake and his three-year-old sister Janet while Howard rested.

He covered his head with a sheet just as the door swung open and two excited kids pounced onto the bed. As usual, Howard pretended to be asleep. At the last second, he flung the sheet back and yelled. The kids knew it was coming but always got a charge out of the jostling. Vivian stood in the doorway with an approving smile. She and the kids loved it almost as much as Howard did.

After five minutes of wrestling, pillow throwing, and just horsing around in general, playtime was over, and it was time for Dad to begin his day. Vivian closed the door, and Howard slipped on his jogging shorts, shoes, and shirt. When he left the house, he assured Janet and Blake that they would have some fun when he returned.

Vivian knew he was scheduled to fly a long mission but didn't know the significance of it or any details. This type of information was classified, and Howard was careful not to divulge information—even to his family. It would be too easy for someone to inadvertently repeat a bit of information and set off a firestorm. Vivian was an ideal wife for a pilot in the Strategic Air Command (SAC), whose bases were located far and wide in most corners of the world. She kept things ship-shape at home by assuming the major job of raising their three young children. Because of her leadership and commitment, Howard was able to devote his full resources to his career—flying a sleek B-47B Stratojet.

When he asked for her opinion about transferring to SAC in 1955, without hesitation she replied, "That's fine with me if that will make you happy because there's nothing worse than a husband coming home unhappy with his work. You do what you think best, and I'll take care of everything at home." That was sufficient for Howard, and after months of training, he was qualified in the B-47B.

Throughout his career, he had flown several different types of propeller-driven aircraft. It was a monumental challenge to transition to a jet with increased speed and different handling characteristics. SAC believed in redundancy and survival. Pilots were required to complete a Radar-Navigation course, which would allow them to continue the mission in the event that the Radar-Navigator became incapacitated. After a rugged survival course, which taught flight crews how to survive in harsh environments in enemy territory, he became an elite SAC pilot.

Vivian viewed moving to different locations as an adventure rather than a hardship. Fortunately, their children quickly adapted to new places and found new friends easily. She was careful not to probe for information but always worried until he returned home safely from a long mission.

Howard and Vivian worked harmoniously as a team. They met while attending Louisville High School in Louisville, Mississippi, where Vivian was a drum majorette and Howard played football. After graduating from high school in 1941, they enrolled at Mississippi State University. Both enjoyed music; Howard played the trombone, and Vivian sang in the orchestra. Howard entered the Civilian Pilot Training Program at MSU and soon earned his private pilot license. He was called to active duty in 1942. He completed flight training in August 1943, pinned on his second lieutenant bars and wings, returned to Mississippi, and married his longtime sweetheart, Vivian Ann.

The outside temperature was a balmy 59 degrees in Homestead, Florida—just right for a four-mile run. He loosened up his six foot, 190 pounds of muscle and bone, then headed down Northwest 9th Avenue, waving at another officer and friend who lived directly across the street. He intercepted and turned south on Krome Avenue, then westbound on 6th Street, where his oldest son Bill attended grade school. Howard hoped that Bill would be outside in his physical education class, but as he approached the school, wiping his forehead with his index finger and glancing at the yard, he saw that the school ground was empty. He felt guilty that he'd been asleep when Bill left for school.

I should be back home early tomorrow morning, he thought, *and I'll make it up by walking to school with him.*

At least that was the plan. Major Richardson and his crew were just a few hours away from a horrifying encounter—one that would test his flying skill, and his B-47B experience, to the limit and beyond.

While Howard continued his morning jog, nearby Homestead Air Force Base buzzed with activity. Airmen prepared his bomber for the next mission. The aircraft crew chief, Technical Sergeant Hubert D. Kidd, had just completed a thorough preflight of the swept wing B-47B and was now simultaneously supervising a refueling crew and providing OJT to his two assistants. Inside a hardened bomb storage building, in a remote part of the base, a three-man crew carefully nudged a black, 7,600-pound thermonuclear bomb onto a dolly. The menacing, flat-nosed Mark 15 Mod 0 thermonuclear bomb, nearly twelve feet long, serial number 47782, was destined for Howard's aircraft.

On another apron of the field, fuel trucks and airmen scurried around several KC-135A Stratotankers, resembling bees attending to their queen. The jet tankers were being fueled and preflighted for a complicated and long training mission called a Uniform Simulated Combat Mission, or USCM. Twenty B-47Bs would be taking to the sky soon, and after reaching altitude, they would need their tanks topped off to replace the fuel expended during start-up, taxi, takeoff, and climb to altitude. Each Stratotanker, capable of carrying 188,000 pounds of JP-4 jet fuel, had only recently arrived at Homestead. They were replacing the faithful, propeller-driven KC-97-L tankers, which held less fuel, were too slow, and were unable to operate at altitudes suitable for the jets.

Howard felt great after the run. He whistled a favorite tune in the shower, recalling yesterday's long USCM briefing. The 19th Bomb Wing at Homestead Air Force Base, located near the southeastern tip of Florida, was being evaluated by a USCM team.

Approximately seventy crew members had gathered in the briefing room a few moments before the briefing was scheduled to begin at 0900 hours sharp. Small groups chatted about various things, such as assignments, promotions, slightly exaggerated golf tales (ditto for fishing stories), and where the next poker game would be held.

At exactly 0900 hours, the operations officer entered the room. "Attention" was called, and all the crew members jumped to their feet as he stepped onto the slightly elevated stage. The operations officer gave a loud "At ease" command, then began his briefing.

A sergeant unfurled two large maps of the eastern U.S., with routes depicted in various colors representing different squadrons. When the men saw the extensive routes on the maps, a low moan emitted across the room and subdued sidebars sprung up. Their assignment was to fly a round robin mission dubbed "Southern Belle." The estimated flight time was calculated to be just slightly under a grueling nine hours. Almost nine hours strapped in the same seat. Add another hour or so for flight preparation, plus more time debriefing and completing paperwork after recovery, and they knew they were in for a long day.

Today's flight must be orchestrated as briefed—on time and with precision. The formidable General Curtis LeMay, former Commander of SAC, was stoking the fires in the Pentagon as Air Force Chief of Staff. His handpicked successor, General Thomas Power, would accept nothing less than perfection. Another motivating factor included high marks by the evaluation team, which was an added plus for a promotion board to consider. Howard had been promoted to major seven years ago in 1951, and he was looking forward to lieutenant colonel. The extra money would be a boon for his growing family, and the higher rank would elevate him into a job of greater responsibility—possibly squadron commander.

His B-47B would be number two in a flight of two aircraft. After refueling over the Gulf of Mexico with a KC-135A, their route would take them northward to a point near the Canadian border, southeast to make a simulated bomb drop at Radford, Virginia, then southbound to Homestead. They were briefed to expect maximum fighter attacks in the simulated enemy area north of Radford, Virginia, where chaff drops and electronic counter measures designed to foul radar were authorized.

After the simulated bomb drop at Radford, Virginia, the bombers would be in friendly territory and enjoy clear sailing back to Homestead, without the pesky fighters running intercepts on them. The weather was forecast to be clear throughout the entire flight, with a full moon. The jet stream was farther south than normal. The meteorologist forecast winds from varying directions up to 120 knots at 35,000 feet. The Radar-Navigators were cautioned to take frequent sextant shots because their aircraft would encounter the U-shaped jet stream from different angles, which would greatly affect their ground speed and headings. It all sounded almost routine; but to Howard, no flight was ever routine. Compliancy or dropping your guard, even for a short time, could result in catastrophic results—especially in a complex, six-engine machine like the B-47B.

In less than four months, there had been two B-47 accidents, which had killed all crew members. One of the accident aircraft had been assigned to the 379th Bombardment Wing at Homestead. It was a shocking occurrence that stunned the entire base for days. On the early morning of October 11, 1957, Captain James D. Butterfield, the aircraft commander, inched the six throttles slightly forward and began taxiing to runway 5 at Homestead Air Force Base after receiving taxi clearance from the ground controller. They were the last aircraft to depart in a formation of four aircraft. Their orders were to fly across the Atlantic Ocean to Wheelus Air Force Base in Libya.

Taxi had begun on time, and everything was going as planned. Sitting behind Butterfield was his co-pilot, 1st Lieutenant John A. Bailey. To Bailey's left sat the aircraft crew chief, Staff Sergeant William A. Washington. Captain Thomas C. Delgado, the Radar-Navigator, was strapped in at his position in the bottom section of the aircraft's nose. In the belly of the aircraft, cradled in its harness, lay a black, bulbous-nosed Mark 6 thermonuclear bomb in ferry configuration. Its nuclear capsule was in a carrying case in the crew compartment, which precluded a nuclear explosion. As they approached runway 5, Butterfield observed the third aircraft takeoff and its lights vanish as it entered a cloud deck at 2,500 feet.

At that time, the crew felt a slight thump emanating from somewhere on the right side of the aircraft. Butterfield believed a tire had blown on the outrigger wheel and advised the tower. Tower cleared them to taxi onto runway 5 and hold while a maintenance crew inspected the tire. It is unclear why the tower wanted the aircraft on an active runway—the only active runway—while they awaited the tire inspection. In any case, the young captain, with only 308 hours in B-47s and 99 hours in the B-47B model and series he was commanding, taxied onto the 11,200 feet-long asphalt runway and stopped. They were scheduled to depart at 0016 EST or 0516 Zulu. No one knows what was discussed inside the cockpit concerning the suspect tire because it was not recorded. Only the conversation with the control tower was recorded. SAC believed in departing and arriving on time. Nothing less was acceptable. It was SAC's culture. Most likely, Captain Butterfield felt pressured to accomplish an on-time departure.

In any case, at 0016 EST, the tower observed the aircraft starting a takeoff roll and received a broken transmission that said, "Will see how it feels rolling" or possibly, "Will check it rolling." When the aircraft was about halfway down the runway, a controller in the tower noticed sparks in the vicinity of the right outrigger wheel and advised the flight crew that the "gear was on fire."

Apparently, when Captain Butterfield heard the word "fire," he pulled the six throttles back to idle to abort the take-off. When he pulled the throttles back and reduced power, this action automatically shut down the water and alcohol injection system that gives the engines extra thrust. Whether or not he engaged the brakes or considered deploying the brake chute is also unknown. Another factor that will never be known is whether the outcome would have been different if the tower controller had described what he saw as "sparks" instead of "fire."

Shortly thereafter, Captain Butterfield must have decided it would be impossible to stop the fully loaded jet before the end of the runway and added full take-off power. It is believed that he did not restart the water/alcohol system. Nearing the end of the runway, he pulled back slightly on the control column to raise the nose, but his airspeed was too slow. The tricycle gear was ripped off when it struck a dike only two feet above sea level, about one quarter mile from the end of the runway. The Stratojet floundered, slammed into the ground, and continued to break-up and burn for another 2,500 feet.

Howard departed on the same runway the following morning. The image of the half-mile long area of charred grass and aircraft parts was burned into his brain.

CHAPTER TWO

Howard pulled on his flight suit and slipped into his highly polished black boots. He always tried to dislodge all thoughts of flying while at home. He recalled a SAC poster in the briefing room that proclaimed, "Enjoy your family while you can. Soar like an eagle on demand."

Vivian prepared his favorite breakfast of French toast, sausage, fresh orange juice, and coffee while their children watched cartoons on a black and white television. The aroma drifted throughout their well kept, three-bedroom bungalow.

As Vivian poured coffee, he placed his arm around her waist, looked deep into her pale blue eyes, and whispered, "Thanks for this great breakfast. It means a lot to me."

She patted his arm and guided him to his chair before plopping down into his lap. "You know I love to cook for my flyboy," she replied coyly.

"Well, good. My next meal will be sometime this evening almost seven miles above terra firma. And it certainly won't compare to this."

She held her cup gracefully with both hands, took a sip, and then said, "Oh, you poor thing."

He smiled, which prompted her to kiss him on the cheek. "Eat before it gets cold," she said, moving to her own chair.

"That was better than eating." He grinned, looking mischievous.

She smiled and asked, "Have you given any more thought to moving on base when housing opens?"

"I've thought about it some. I'm not sure if the base school will be open by then. Bill seems to enjoy his current school. If we moved on base and the base school wasn't open, he could be transferred to another school. Of course, moving on base would solve the transportation problem, and maybe we could keep our home and rent it."

"How's that?"

"I believe we could keep it rented if we only charged enough for payments, taxes, insurance, and upkeep. It would be nice to have a piece of property pay for itself.

"If we moved on base, I could leave the Chieftian with you when I'm flying. But if we stay here, I could buy something small, maybe a used MG to drive back and forth to work. There are usually some very good bargains on base when lower ranking personnel are transferred overseas, since the Air Force doesn't pay for shipping the vehicle." He frowned. "I don't like leaving you here alone without transportation."

"Our neighbors would help in an emergency."

"That's true, but I still prefer that you have your own vehicle."

She smiled. "You're sweet."

Howard swallowed a bite of sausage and said, in an exaggerated southern drawl, "Guess it's just that good ol' Mississippi charm."

They both laughed as Vivian squeezed the strong arm of her chisel-faced, thirty-six-year-old husband, who could easily have been confused with Robert Mitchum.

After breakfast, they took time to play a game of croquet in the back yard. The temperature had climbed to sixty-eight gorgeous degrees under clear skies. Blake and Janet assisted Howard in setting up the goal stakes and wickets, although they could barely lift a mallet. But that was part of the fun. After the game, everyone sat around a table on the patio laughing and drinking freshly squeezed lemonade.

Soon, it was time for Howard to begin his journey to Homestead Air Force Base, which was located about seven miles east of their home on Northwest 9th Avenue. He grabbed his hat, leather jacket, and sunglasses as the kids quietly observed. He kneeled down to kiss them good-by, noticing that their eyes were sad.

"Be good, mind Mom, and I'll see you soon," he said softly.

Vivian opened the door for him. "Where's your thermos, fly-boy?" she said, smiling. He had obtained the thermos, designed for a B-47B aircraft, through a friend in the supply department. It allowed him to enjoy Vivian's coffee instead of the coffee supplied by the Air Force.

He shrugged, then laughed as Vivian drew the thermos from behind her back and handed it to him; they embraced, and he strolled smartly to the carport where the family's blue 1954 Pontiac Chieftain awaited. She hurried to the car as Howard shut the door, leaned inside, and kissed him. "Be careful and hurry home," she said, her voice unsteady.

"Don't worry," Howard said. "I promise you I will."

The huge, flat eight engine came to life after the first revolution of the starter. He backed out of the driveway, waved to his family, and then pressed down on the accelerator, making the rear tires chirp as it lurched forward.

That's not like her, he thought. *She had tears in her eyes, and her voice seemed . . . different, fearful.*

Howard was scheduled to depart at 4:51 Eastern Time or 2151 Zulu. He normally arrived at base operation in the neighborhood of one hour before scheduled departure time. He had left home a few minutes early because of the anticipated delay entering the base. After stopping at the intersection of busy Krome Avenue, he waited for a chance to cross. He reached over, turned on the radio, and pressed a chrome button for a pre-selected station. The radio hummed for a few seconds while the tubes warmed up, then it came alive.

"You're listening to the Armed Forces Radio and Television Service, AFRTS. The race for space is heating up. The Soviet News Agency Tass announced today that Sputnik reentered the earth's atmosphere last month, disintegrated, and burned up after making fourteen hundred earth orbits. You may recall the successful launch of their second satellite last November. The Soviets claim their latest satellite has a dog on board and that it's fairing well in the half-ton satellite orbiting 900 miles above earth.

"The U.S. entered the race last Friday with the launch of its first satellite from Cape Canaveral called Explorer I. The 30.8-pound Explorer I is equipped with devices for measuring cosmic radiation, external temperature, micrometeorite impact, and erosion as well as two half-pound radios. Dr. William Pickering, head of

the Jet Propulsion Laboratory at the California Institute of Technology, disclosed that cosmic radiation in the orbit of Explorer I is only twelve times that on the earth's surface and no great barrier to human space flight. Last month, President Eisenhower asked Congress to make an additional 1.37 billion dollars available in the current fiscal year to speed up and expand missile and air defenses. Meanwhile, Vice President Nixon suggested that bombers rather than missiles will be the decisive strategic weapon for an appreciable time."

Howard smiled, nodding his head in agreement.

"Today, the president directed his science adviser, James Killan Jr., to study and report on whether a civilian or a military agency should head U.S. space activities.

"The controversial issue of nuclear weapons has surfaced again."

Howard reached over and turned up the volume.

"Just last month, Canadian Defense Minister G. R. Pearkes told the House of Commons in Ottawa that U.S. aircraft carry nuclear weapons over Canada, but only under specific circumstances and with written advance permission from Canada. Early today, Britain's Acting Prime Minster contradicted earlier announcements that British-based U.S. bombers fly regular patrols with nuclear weapons. R. A. Butler told Parliament that U.S. jets carry nuclear weapons over Britain only in special operational exercises"

Howard smiled and rolled his eyes.

"The Soviet Union has invited the United States to send several observers to its elections for the Supreme Soviet next month. The U.S. will accept the invitation, reciprocating the visit of Soviet observers in our 1956 elections. The Senate has unanimously passed an emergency defense appropriations bill, which will provide

funds to expedite construction of Strategic Air Command bases, and for missile programs and civil air defenses.

"The Pentagon released more details today on the tragic military aircraft accident that occurred last Friday shortly after 1900 hours Pacific. An Air Force C-118A with thirty-five military passengers and six crew members aboard collided over Norwalk California with a Navy P2-V with eight reservists aboard. The only survivors were two crew members on the P2-V. Miraculously, only one civilian was killed in the heavily populated suburb of Los Angeles when the debris fell to the ground. A spokesman from the Pentagon said both aircraft were operating under the see-and-be-seen rule, which is a common procedure in good weather conditions. The pilots of both aircraft assumed responsibility for separation rather than air traffic controllers.

"Another unfortunate accident between two Air Force jets occurred yesterday near the Savannah River Project. An Air Force spokesman told AFRTS that two F-86L fighter aircraft based at Charleston, South Carolina collided while conducting practice intercepts. One pilot ejected safely, but the pilot of the other jet perished. Another jet was damaged but was able to return safely to Charleston Air Force Base. Name and rank of the pilots were not released.

"And now for some good news I'm sure you've been waiting for. House Armed services Commission Chairman Carl Vinson, Democrat from Georgia, introduced a bill last month to provide 518 million dollars in pay raises for armed force members at the request of the Defense Department.

"That wraps up the military news. And now we begin thirty minutes of uninterrupted music to entertain our hard working military family. Kicking it off is Sonny James and his smash hit, 'Young Love.'"

I wonder how much of that 518 million I'll receive? I'll be thankful for any raise but wish it could be more. Hope to save enough for the kids' formal education, give them the opportunity to attend an exclusive university. Maybe I should have followed the path of my dad and twin brother, David. Funny, David still refers to me as his womb-mate . . . I could have entered the medical field where the big bucks roam. But flying's in my blood. It's been there ever since that first ride with a barnstormer in a pasture near Louisville . . . Just a kid but finally convinced Dad to let me ride. That pilot strutting about in his goggles and boots as locals gawked, noise from the engine, smell of oil and gas, wind in my face . . . I was hooked at that moment . . . and still am. Down deep I know I wouldn't want to do anything else.

Howard turned off the main highway into the entrance to Homestead Air Force Base and fell in line with several other vehicles waiting for authorization to enter. He glanced over at the latest SAC billboard placed strategically so that a passerby and those entering the base would have trouble missing it. The billboard depicted a departing B-47B at liftoff with its water and alcohol injection system in full bloom. Emblazoned on the billboard in large letters was SAC's proclamation, "Peace Is Our Profession." Nodding his head in agreement, he thought, *Without us, those Russkies would be over here in a New York instant.*

The Air Police guarding the main entrance gate were always scrupulous, but today extra vigilance was clearly evident. They couldn't chance an evaluator to enter the highly classified Strategic Air Command Base without proper authorization, or perhaps carrying a simulated explosive device hidden in their automobile.

The driver and all passengers were required to exit each vehicle. The trunk, engine compartment, and interior were given a thorough inspection by an AP while another AP inspected beneath the vehicles using a mirror attached to a handle. Howard turned off the radio as he inched forward. A low flying B-47B screamed overhead, shaking the ground, belching kerosene smoke and steam from the injection system and temporarily drowning out any conversation with the APs.

His thoughts drifted to his upcoming flight. It should be similar to many others he had flown. But no flight is ever routine in a complicated machine like the six-engine B-47B, with three crew members coordinating their actions—especially one being evaluated and carrying an expensive thermonuclear bomb.

Finally, he was cleared to enter Homestead. He proceeded to base operations and parked the Chieftain. As he entered base operations, he noticed his co-pilot, First Lieutenant Robert Lagerstrom, studying a weather chart. Howard walked over to Lagerstrom, set down his thermos, and clapped him on the shoulder. Lagerstrom turned and grinned. "Afternoon, Major," he said, raising his voice to be heard over the clanking teletype machines, which were spewing out weather reports. "Good to see you, sir."

"Same here, Bob. Ready for a sight seeing tour of the countryside?"

"Yes, sir. I'm jumping at the bit. Ready to go. Need the flight time."

Howard retrieved a DD175 Aircraft Clearance form from a shelf and placed it on a slanted piece of plexiglas. A navigation map of the eastern United Stated was inserted underneath the plexiglas. Weather charts of various types and size hung on every wall. He began filling in the blanks on the DD175. Glancing around, he wondered why Captain Winters, his Radar-Navigator, wasn't present.

Strange. Normally he shows up early.

The Radar-Navigator is an essential crew member responsible for navigation, bombing, photographic, and radar rendezvous functions in coordination with the pilot and co-pilot.

"Have you seen Captain Winters?"

"No, sir. Haven't seen him since our last mission."

Howard thought highly of Bob. His easy-going nature, pleasant personality, and boyish looks made him a favorite around the base. He was very professional and competent in the cockpit—the kind of copilot needed in an emergency or unusual situation when quick thinking and good judgment is paramount. But he needed more time as pilot-in-command. Bob had only logged 553.2 total flight hours. His total time in the B-47B was 176.3 hours, and 107.6 hours of that time was performed as aircraft commander. Howard gave control of the aircraft to the young lieutenant at every opportunity in hopes of elevating him to aircraft commander and then promotion to captain.

Howard had accumulated over 3,000 hours, many of them combat missions during WWII over France and Germany. He'd completed a staggering thirty-five combat missions flying a B-17G, christened *The Mississippi Miss,* without a single loss of life. On June 5, 1944, he flew five hours dropping bombs to soften up fortified German positions along the French Coast. On June 6, D-Day, he spent thirteen hours in the air bombing targets in Caen and Argetan, France. Allegedly, *The Mississippi*

Miss had suffered so much flak damage during her thirty-five missions that only half of her original fuselage skin remained intact.

Howard had also logged over a thousand hours in the B-47B both as aircraft commander and as an instructor pilot.

Due to the USCM mission, the room was unusually crowded with crew members completing their paperwork.

Bob looked up from his paperwork. "The assistant ops officer, Captain Everett Robinson, has some information for you."

"Any indication as to what the subject is?"

"No, sir. Just said he needed to see you when you arrive."

"Okay, thanks. While I see what's on his mind, take a look at the 365F weight and balance. I want us to complete the paperwork before the weather briefing scheduled for 1545."

"Yes, sir. I'll get right on it."

When Howard entered the office, Captain Robinson was updating aircraft and crew member status information on a Plexiglas tote board using various colored grease pencils. Howard nodded to another captain sitting next to Robinson's desk, who was holding several documents in his hand. Howard cleared his throat. "Have something for me, Captain Robinson?"

Captain Robinson twirled around, glancing at Howard's name plate and rank.

"Good afternoon, Major Richardson. Yes, sir, Captain Winters is on sick call."

Robinson glanced at the officer sitting next to his desk. "This is Captain Leland Woolard from the 28th Bomb Squadron. He was called in by your squadron CO to replace Captain Winters. Captain Woolard is in the process of reviewing your pre-flight plan aircraft performance, pilot flight progress chart, navigation, and bombing data."

Captain Woolard rose from his chair, and Howard extended his arm and shook hands with him. Leland was a large man, a tad taller than Howard. His hair had receded slightly on his forehead, and dark circles under his eyes made him look older than he actually was.

His hand's clammy. Seems a bit nervous. Hope this gent knows his stuff. Bad timing with the USCM eval in progress. Try to make him feel welcome and relaxed.

"Pleased to meet you, Captain Woolard," he said. "And welcome to the 30th."

"Glad to assist, sir."

"Did you attend yesterday's USCM briefing?"

"Yes, sir, I did."

"Excellent. First Lieutenant Bob Lagerstrom is the copilot. He's finalizing some of the paperwork. We're scheduled to depart at 1651 hours. Our weather briefing is scheduled for 1545, which makes it a bit tight, time-wise, to complete our preflight and depart as scheduled. Immediately after the briefing, we'll pick up our gear and head for the flight line. I'll fill you in with more details at the flight line briefing."

"Sounds like a good plan.

"Have you met Bob?"

"I've seen him around but don't really know him."

Howard glanced at Captain Robinson and said, "Thanks for your help, Captain." As he headed for the door, he turned to Leland and said, "Let's go meet Bob and see if he needs assistance."

As they worked their way across the busy room toward Bob, Howard quizzed Leland in a casual manner designed to loosen him up and make him feel welcome as an important, integral part of the team.

"How long have you been at Homestead?"

"About six months. Just beginning to know my way around the base and the local area."

"Know what you mean. Seems like we just get settled in an area and orders are automatically printed transferring us to another location."

They both laughed, which is exactly what Howard wanted.

Leland looked more at ease. "You a golfer?" he asked.

"Knock some balls around occasionally. How about you?"

"Love the stupid game. Drives me crazy sometimes, but can't wait to get back on the course and punish myself again."

Howard grinned, patted Leland on his back, and said, "We'd make a good pair. Tell you what. I'll give you a call next time the gang plays a round."

"Sounds great, Major." He unzipped a pocket on his flight suit, pulled out a card, and offered it to Howard. "Here's my number. Call anytime. If I'm not on duty, I'll be there. Rain or shine."

Howard laughed. "I believe I've found another golfer that's almost as crazy about the game as I am."

They approached Bob, and Howard made the introductions. After some quick pleasantries, Bob continued his work on weight and balance, a critical safety portion of the flight planning. Howard resumed filling in the blanks on the DD175 Aircraft Clearance Form. Under section B, Occupants, he struck through Captain Winters' name and gave the form to Leland to enter his name, serial number, and other data. In section C, Flight Plan, Howard entered N/A for an alternate airport, but in section D, Weather, he entered MacDill Air Force Base as an alternate. In the remarks section, he entered NOPAR to the 20th, 30th, 31st, 37th, and 5th Air Divisions. This meant that the CAA controllers were forbidden to forward Howard's flight plan to the Air Defense Command radar sites in those air divisions. The five air divisions listed encompassed airspace overlying a vast area from Arkansas to North Dakota, eastward to New York, and back to Arkansas. The 35th Air Division, which encompassed the southeastern United States, was not included because the 19th Bomb Wing was briefed that no other intercepts or activity would take place south of Radford, Virginia. He signed and dated the form February 4, 1958, as aircraft commander.

Bob gave Howard and Leland a flight lunch request form, then said in a joking voice, "Think we should ask for steak and potatoes?"

Howard laughed heartily. "Great idea," he said. "Hope it works, but don't count on it. You might end up with only a note saying 'your steak's on the way.'"

Bob blushed and said, "They say it doesn't hurt to dream." His countenance turned serious. "Sir, I'm ready to brief you concerning the weight and balance."

"Okay, Bob. Leland, I'd like you to observe carefully. The more knowledge you absorb about the mission, the better. By the way, Leland has started reviewing Captain Winter's paperwork. But he may need some help from you, Bob. That's a lot of information to digest in such a short time."

"Sure. Glad to help any way I can."

Howard and Leland stood on either side of Bob as he explained his calculations. "This aircraft is equipped with heavy duty 32-ply tires. Our operating weight is 85,502 pounds. One hundred rounds of 20-millimeter ammo weighs 630 pounds. A full load of chaff equals 650 pounds." He paused, cleared his throat, and then continued. "We're carrying one Mark 15 Mod 0 bomb at 7,600 pounds. Fuel, 67,800 pounds built in; 9,500 pounds in the bomb bay; and 22,000 external in the drop tanks for a total of 99,300 pounds. The water injection fluid weighs 4,820 pounds. Takeoff condition before corrections comes to 197,752 pounds. I calculate engine start, taxi, and the takeoff roll will use 1,100 pounds of fuel out of the forward main tank; 1,100 pounds out of the center main tank; 1,155 pounds out of the aft main tank; and 3,400 pounds of water injection fluid for a total of 6,755 pounds. Our corrected takeoff condition is 190,997 pounds. This includes our weight and the weight of our gear. It's well below the maximum flight gross weight of 221,000 pounds, and the center of gravity is within acceptable limits. Estimated landing condition will be well below the gross landing weight of 125,000 pounds, and center of gravity will be within acceptable tolerance."

Bob looked up at Howard for his reaction. Howard nodded an okay.

Bob signed the form then gave it to Howard. He glanced over the figures again and signed it as H. Richardson, Maj.

Howard handed the form back to Bob. "Good work," he said. "I've got to sign the custodian receipt for the weapon and talk to the aircraft commander of Ivory 1 if I have time. Now that we have the weight pegged, you can complete the DD175 and turn it in. I'll be back in time for the weather briefing."

"Yes, sir."

After Howard left, Leland turned to Bob. In a hushed tone, just above the din of the noisy room, he said, "I've never flown with Major Richardson. Could you tell me a little about him? What he expects in the cockpit?"

"Sure. He's all business when he straps in, and that's the way I like it. Major Richardson is strict but fair. If he makes a mistake, which is rare, he'll admit it and not blame a subordinate. I like flying with him.

He gives me the controls at every opportunity. He flew thirty-five combat missions over Germany and France without losing a crew member. That in itself tells me a great deal about the man. You do your job, and he won't interfere with you. He's arguably the most competent B-47B pilot and instructor pilot at Homestead. If we should be so unfortunate some day to carry out a strike against the Soviet Union, he'd be the pilot I'd like to have in the front seat."

"That's good to know. I'm looking forward to flying with him—and thanks, Bob, for being candid."

Bob nodded. "You're welcome, Captain Woolard."

Howard entered the area. "Bob, is the DD175 ready?"

"Yes it is, Major. Want a review?"

"Go ahead. Then we'll go over to the meteorologist office for our briefing."

Bob began. "An IFR flight plan was filed yesterday with the Civil Aeronautics Administration using the Southern Belle route. Our radio call is Ivory 2. Total distance is 3,527 nautical miles. Estimated time en route is eight hours and thirty-five minutes. True air speed is 425 knots. I reviewed the NOTAMs, specifically for the Warning Areas in the Gulf, which are not in use during our scheduled time for air refueling. And the final item, our take-off distance, using 60 degrees temperature, is 7,900 feet."

Howard quickly reviewed the numbers, which he knew were well within the ballpark, then signed his name in the "Signature of Clearing Authority" column.

CHAPTER THREE

The weather briefing was short and basically a rehash of the previous day. Clear, with unlimited visibility along the entire route, strong jet stream dipping farther south than normal, and a full moon after darkness. They walked down a hall with offices on either side to a locker room where their gear was stored. Each airman had been issued a personal parachute, Mae West, dinghy, helmet with an attached oxygen mask, professional kit, leather gloves and jacket, arctic clothing, and a flashlight with fresh batteries.

Before they departed the locker room, Howard verified that Leland and Bob possessed all the required items. They collected their gear, carried it outside, and loaded it on a blue 1956 Air Force issue Dodge truck with a brown canvas cover over the bed and serial numbers stenciled on the doors. They hopped in the truck and took a seat on a wooden board on either side of the bed for the ride to the aircraft. The driver confirmed that their flight lunches were on the truck.

Howard glanced over his shoulder at the distant flight line where several rows of perfectly aligned B-47s and KC-135s awaited their masters. The sleek B-47s, with their swept-back wings, slanted vertical stabilizers, and slightly elevated noses gave the illusion of motion even when parked. A chill ran down Howard's back as he gazed at the aircraft, described by some as war machines, but were in fact the front line of defense for the U.S.—the difference between freedom and probable annihilation.

The truck stopped near a B-47B. Emblazoned on both sides of the vertical stabilizer were the numbers 12349. Two guards with serious expressions, armed with automatic weapons, stepped forward. The larger of the two, bearing three stripes on his sleeves, was obviously in charge.

"Exit the vehicle and present proper identification," he demanded, stepping forward. The guards' job was to ensure that the top-secret bomb was secure until the flight crew assumed responsibility. After the guards accepted their identity, Howard entered the bomb bay and verified the serial number on the bomb's fin. It matched the serial number, 47782, entered on his copy of the Atomic Energy Commission's Temporary Custodian Receipt. He took custody and responsibility for the bomb. The guards snapped to, gave Howard a salute, and departed, relieved that someone else was now responsible for the bomb.

Hubert directed his two assistants to help the driver unload the air crew's gear, placing it neatly in separate stacks near the lowered entrance ladder.

Leland, Bob, and Hubert formed a line facing Howard. Howard began the briefing. "Gentlemen, let's review the emergency procedures and the mission before beginning the inspections.

"If bailout becomes necessary, I'll give the order by one long ring on the alarm bell and announce loudly over the interphone, 'bailout-ejection seats.' Bob should acknowledge, followed by Leland. The preferred method is the ejection seats. If they are not available or inoperative, use the escape chute. Next in priority is Leland's downward ejection hatch opening. That's assuming Leland has ejected. I'll try to slow to less than 200 indicated air speed, time permitting. If we need to eject below 2,000 feet above the surface, Bob and I should unfasten our safety belts to aid in rapid separation from the seat after ejection. As a last resort, assuming everything else fails, I'll jettison the canopy, and we'll jump over the side. Any questions?"

No one spoke. Ejection procedures were one item the crew members knew by heart, and they were keenly aware of the potential problem with ejection at low altitude—especially for the Radar-Navigator, whose seat would eject downward. That meant there was less time for the parachute to unfurl and safely deliver the airman to the surface. Howard had given thought to this scenario many times and decided that if time and circumstances permitted, he would bank the aircraft steeply as he issued the ejection order, which would hopefully provide added safety for the Radar-Navigator.

Howard continued. "To quickly review our mission, we'll be number two in a flight of two, departing at 2151 Zulu." He turned and pointed to a B-47B parked on the adjacent flight line with airmen in the process of finalizing an exterior inspection.

"That's our lead aircraft, Ivory 1."

We're a tad late, Howard thought. *Got to proceed smartly but safely.*

"Ivory 1 will be squawking IFF on mode 2. Our IFF will remain on standby.

"Air-refuel will be at angels 31 over the Gulf of Mexico with our tanker Shell 7, then proceed northbound to the Canadian border. Expect fighter interceptors approaching the Eastern ADIZ. Those scope-dopes don't know anything about our mission and will scramble fighters if they detect us on their radar." The three chuckled about the manner in which Howard referred to the Air Defense Command Controllers.

"Next, we'll turn southeastbound toward our target at Radford, Virginia. Bob, I recommend you spend some time practicing with the A5 fire control system. There should be plenty of opportunities."

Bob acknowledged by nodding his head and smiling faintly.

"Fighter types expected are the F-86, F-102, and possibly the F-104. We'll need about five minutes between us and Ivory 1 over the target to give the bomb plot crew sufficient time to set up their equipment for us after Ivory 1 makes their simulated drop. We'll reduce our airspeed and maybe dogleg some to acquire the necessary spacing. Our profile over the bomb run will be at 460 knots true at angels 38. Two minutes after the bomb run, we'll descend to angels 35 and resume normal speed. After passing Radford, we'll be back in friendly territory and absent any fighter attacks. Our IFF will be on standby on all modes the entire flight. Questions?"

Leland cleared his throat and asked, "When do we climb to angels 38 and increase speed?"

"Good question, Leland. We start the climb and increase speed so as to be in the profile at least five minutes prior to the target. Anything else?"

No one spoke.

"Okay. Leland, give us a time hack, and we'll be ready for the interior inspection."

Leland held up his left arm, pushed back his sleeve, and watched closely as the second hand moved on his Air Force issue watch. "At my mark, it'll be 2102 . . . five, four, three, two, one, mark—2102 Zulu."

"Sergeant Kidd, let me see the Aircraft Status and Discrepancies form and the Maintenance Preflight Inspection worksheet."

"Yes, sir," Hubert said, stepping forward. He handed the papers to Howard.

Howard carefully examined the forms and remarked, "Nothing wrong with this bird. Good job, Sergeant."

Hubert smiled. "Thank you, sir."

"Bob, it's yours."

"Thank you, sir." Bob removed the Before Interior Inspection Checklist from his professional kit and called out the items followed by Howard's response.

"ATO safety devices."

"As required. JATO not used."

"Station inspection."

"Completed."

"Briefing."

"Completed."

"Equipment check."

"Completed."

"Life raft."

Howard paused, looking at Hubert.

"Mark IV four-man life raft checked and properly installed."

"Checked."

"Bob, since our route takes us over water and because it's your responsibility to release the life raft, I want you to review the emergency procedures before we get our feet wet."

Bob acknowledged, "Wilco, Major," then continued. "External power."

Howard glanced at the power receptacle and responded, "Off."

"Major Richardson, that concludes this inspection checklist."

Howard looked at his watch as he stepped on the first rung of the entrance ladder, then looked over his shoulder and said, "Bob, let's complete the interior inspection while Leland sets up his equipment."

"Yes, sir." Bob replaced the Before Interior Inspection Checklist and grabbed the checklist labeled Interior Preflight Inspection.

Entering the cockpit, Bob called out the checklist items and Howard responded.

"Bailout spoiler."

"Installed."

While Howard and Bob carried out the interior inspection, Leland donned his parachute and began loading his personal gear into his Radar-Navigator position located in the bottom portion of the aircraft's nose.

Bob continued with the checklist.

"Bailout spoiler air bottle."

"Checked."

"Main AC power shield."

"Checked."

"Hand ax."

"Stowed."

"First aid kits."

"Checked."

"Fire extinguisher."

"Checked."

"Forward walk around oxygen bottle."

"Checked."

At this point in the inspection, the roles reversed. Howard took the checklist, called out the item, and Bob performed the function and responded.

"Let-down books and facility charts."

Bob opened the data case, thumbed through the documents, and verified that the current navigational charts, pilot handbooks, and weight and balance handbook were present.

"Checked."

"Aft walk around oxygen bottle."

"Checked."

"ECM switches."

Bob leaned over and closely eyed the Electronic Countermeasure Panel on the starboard side of the co-pilot's station.

"Off."

"Chaff dispenser switches."

"Off."

"Canopy emergency jettison air bottle."

"Checked."

"G-files and loose equipment."

"Checked."

"Gunnery system."

Bob glanced aft of the co-pilot station at the Turret Control Panel to verify the location of the gun safety switch. "Switch off and safe."

"Circuit breakers."

"Checked."

"Ejection seats."

Both Howard and Bob inspected six items on their seats, then responded. "Checked."

"Periscopic port."

"Closed."

"Emergency turn and bank."

Howard, then Bob responded, "Checked and normal."

They continued the extensive checklist, covering items such as the approach chute deployment switches, gear levers, throttles, and fuel tank jettison switches.

Next on the list was the critical DC power system, which dictated mandatory abortion of the mission if either bus failed to take the DC load. When checked, both buses were satisfactory.

Bob contacted Hubert on the interphone and said, "Sergeant Kidd, connect the external DC power."

"Roger, connecting DC power." After a short pause while he inserted the heavy plug into the side of the aircraft, Hubert replied, "On the line."

The remaining thirty-five items for the interior preflight inspection were checked, including the critical systems: oxygen, fuel, hydraulic, air refueling, ELGE, controls, flaps, instruments, radios, and the gunnery fire-control.

"Good job, Bob. Let's do the exterior," Howard said, as he climbed down the ladder.

Bob grabbed the Exterior Inspection Checklist from his Professional Equipment Bag and followed Howard down the ladder.

Bob sensed Howard's time concern and promptly began the inspection as Hubert joined them.

"External DC power."

"As required."

"Left pitot cover."

Howard removed the red streamer labeled "Remove before flight" from the pitot tube, held it up in Bob's view, and replied, "Removed."

"Nose window and bombsight."

"Clean and unbroken."

"Static ports."

"Clear."

"Radome."

"Flush and latched."

As they approached the aft right side wheel well, Howard questioned Hubert. "Sergeant, are the boost pump drains within fuel leakage limits?"

"Yes, sir," Hubert replied. "They were well within limits yesterday at the completion of my post flight, about 1600 hours."

"Thank you."

"Right forward main boost pump."

"Checked."

They continued the inspection, covering one hundred and twenty-five additional items, including wheels and tires, external wing tank fuel quantity and filler neck, aileron, flaperon, trim tabs, flaps, camera, rudder, elevator, ammunition cans, and brake chute.

"Exterior inspection complete," Bob announced.

"Good job, men. Bob, let's gather our gear and get aboard."

CHAPTER FOUR

Howard and Bob donned their parachute. When Howard entered the aircraft, the strong odor of jet fumes irritated his nostrils and throat. Several nearby aircraft were performing their engine run-up, and with little or no wind, the fumes dissipated slowly. He noted that Leland was wearing his helmet and oxygen mask.

"Bob, due to the high level of carbon monoxide, let's don our oxygen mask and set at one hundred percent. When we're airborne, remind me to reset to normal. We don't want to waste our oxygen."

"Yes, sir," Bob replied. "I'll make a mental note of it." He donned his helmet and slipped on his leather jacket and gloves. They connected their mike cords and plugged the oxygen hoses into the receptacle.

When Howard plugged his oxygen hose into the receptacle and adjusted the selector switch, all three crew members were able to communicate with each other through the interphone.

Howard climbed into his seat, thumbed the mike switch on his control wheel, and stated, "Interphone check."

Bob and Leland responded, "Loud and clear."

"Leland, due to heavy fumes, use 100% oxygen."

"Roger that, sir. Already on 100%."

Howard smiled and thought, *Hmm, I believe Leland will be a good crew member. I like people who think for themselves.*

"Bob, Before Starting Engines Checklist, please."

"Roger. Ejection seat and canopy safety pins. All crew members report."

The three crew members responded, "Streamers and pins removed."

"Safety belt and shoulder harness."

"Fastened."

"Controls."

Howard and Bob unlatched their control column by pulling with their left hand, unlocked the disconnect handle by pressing the thumb button, and pulled the column farther back to engage it. After the disconnect handle slid down into the engaged position, both responded, "Engaged."

"Mike cord, mask, and bailout bottle."

"Connected."

"Oxygen check."

Each crew member checked pressure, flow blinker and hose connections, and responded, "Oxygen check complete, pressure normal and warning switch on."

"Canopy jettison handle."

Howard and Bob verified the handles were in place, covers closed, and then transmitted, "In place."

"Parking brake."

Howard glances at the Brake Lock Knob and announced, "Set."

"Bomb door switch."

"Off."

"Fire shutoff switches."

Howard pushed on each of the six push-to-test warning lights mounted along the top of his instrument panel, one for each engine, and responded, "Depressed."

"Gear lever, indicator, and ELGE lights."

Howard and Bob observed the lever to verify its down position, lights out in the lever tip, and four down indicators showing on the instrument panel. Bob turned and looked over his left shoulder at the ELGE stand to verify illumination of four green lights and to ensure the red unsafe-to-land light was not on.

Howard and Bob responded, "Lever and four down."

"Throttles."

Howard then Bob transmitted, "Cutoff."

"Water injection switches."

"Off."

"Radios and IFF."

Howard turned to his right where the radio and IFF panel was located, turned the radios on for warm-up and the IFF master switch to stand-by. He unfolded his JN-45N jet navigation chart, then located

Miami. He noted the Miami omni frequency as 113.4, dialed in the numbers, rotated the course selector knob 360 degrees, and replied, "On, and stand-by."

"Bomb door locks and gear locks."

Howard glanced to his left, where a ground crew member displayed the locks. He transmitted to Hubert, "In sight, stow."

"Alternators."

"Reset and off."

"Circuit breakers."

"In."

"Radio call."

Bob turned the UHF and liaison radio volume up, then selected Homestead control tower frequency. The frequency was busy. but when a break came, he transmitted. "Tower, Ivory 2, radio check."

"Ivory 2 loud and clear."

He kept the radio on tower frequency but turned down the volume.

"Brake chute deploy and jettison handles."

Howard and Bob replies, "Both checked."

"Fuel control panel."

Howard selected TME for the number two engine and TE for the other five engines and transmitted, "Set."

"That completes the Before Starting Engine Checklist.

"Roger, let's complete the Starting Engine Checklist."

Bob secured the Starting Engine Checklist and began:

"Ignition switches."

Without hesitation, Howard glanced to the right side of the cockpit and, with his right index finger, flipped the six toggle switches upward from the Off to Normal position and transmitted, "Normal." He was extremely familiar with each of the dozens of switches, knobs, wheels, and buttons in the cockpit. He knew their position, what they felt like, and could locate them blindfolded if necessary.

"Ready to start engines."

Howard transmitted, "Stand by to start engines."

Hubert responded, "Clear to start and fire guard on number four."

Bob positioned the DC voltmeter selector to number four engine and transmitted, "DC voltmeter selector on number four."

"Start engine."

For extra safety, Howard looked to his right to verify that the fire guard was clear of the engine intake, turned the Starter Selector switch from Off to number four engine, pushed the spring loaded Starter Switch to Start for two seconds, then released it.

Bob closely observed his instruments, then transmitted, "Voltage up. RPM six percent."

Howard advanced the throttle to Start for number four engine and watched as the EGT rose, indicating a successful start. After a short pause while the EGT stabilized around 650 degrees centigrade, he increased the throttle to 40 percent RPM.

"Ready to start number five."

Approximately thirty seconds after Howard pressed the Start switch, Bob transmitted, "Low RPM, negative combustion." He sounded concerned.

CHAPTER FIVE

Howard immediately moved the starter switch to Cutoff, closed number five throttle, and transmitted in a somewhat disappointed tone, "Negative start. We'll give the starter time to cool and hopefully start number five last."

The remaining four engines started normally. Number five started on the second attempt. "Before Taxi Checklist," Howard transmitted, relieved.

"Hydraulic pressure and quantity," Bob said.

"Checked."

"Entrance door."

Bob verified that the pressure door was up and the hook seated.

"Checked."

This was a critical item. Hubert observed the door, moved his hand over the latch, then transmitted, "Entrance ladder stowed; door closed and latched."

Howard glanced anxiously at his watch. It read 2133.

Cutting the time too close—especially during an eval. Weather briefing fouled our schedule.

"Clear bomb doors."

Howard looked down at Hubert. "Verify clear to close."

Hubert glanced up at Howard. "Bomb bay doors clear to close."

Howard instructed Leland to close the door switch, and for Hubert to verify when the doors were closed and latched.

After approximately one minute, Leland reported, "Doors closed," followed by Hubert, "Doors closed and latched."

This was another critical item, and for a double verification, Howard briefly looked at the left side of his instrument panel, where the bomb door position indicator was located, to verify its position.

"External power."

Howard looked over his shoulder at Hubert and transmitted, "Sergeant, remove external power, wheel chocks, disconnect ground interphone."

Hubert keyed his mike and replied, "Have a safe flight, gentlemen." His assistants quickly performed the tasks and placed the equipment on the port side of the aircraft in Howard's view.

"Removed and in sight."

"Power control."

"On, lights out."

"Steering ratio selector."

Howard moved the rudder pedals with his feet until they were neutralized, reached forward, placed his right hand on the Steering Ratio Selector, and moved it to the TAXI detent position.

"Taxi detent."

"IFF."

"Set, on standby."

"Before Taxi Checklist complete except for crew chief clearance and parking brake."

Howard acknowledged Bob and selected the aircraft-to-aircraft UHF frequency, thumbed the transmitter, and advised Ivory 1, "Ivory 2 ready to taxi."

"Ivory 2, roger; switch to ground freq."

He changed the radio frequency to ground control and transmitted, "Two" to let Ivory 1 know he was monitoring the frequency.

The co-pilot of Ivory 1 contacted Homestead ground control. "Ground, Ivory 1, flight of two at tango; ready to taxi, IFR to Homestead."

"Ivory 1, roger; taxi to runway five. Follow the two 135 tankers turning out of golf for the taxiway. Wind calm, altimeter 3016. Standby for IFR clearance."

"Ivory 1, roger."

Howard jotted down the info on his knee-pad, then keyed his mike and responded, "Two," as he dialed in 3016 in his altimeter.

Bob responded, "3016," as he set the altimeter and verified its reading of 6 feet, the elevation of the Homestead airport above sea level.

When Ivory 1 moved forward, Howard signaled to Hubert that he was ready to taxi. Hubert waved a hand-held wand, green light illuminated, followed by a snappy salute. Howard returned the salute, then depressed the left rudder to release the parking brake, adding power to all six engines until movement was noted before slightly reducing to taxi power. As they began taxiing toward runway 5, Bob called out the While Taxiing Checklist.

"Brakes and steering."

"Checked."

"Hydraulic pressure and quantity."

"Checked."

"Turn and bank."

Howard, then Bob reported, "Checked."

"Directional gyro."

Bob responded, "Checked." He made a mental note to verify and, if necessary, reset the gyro once they were lined up on runway 5.

"Steering ratio."

A controller in the tower transmitted, "Ground, IFR clearance for Ivory 1 and flight."

Howard grabbed his pencil and copied the clearance on his knee-pad.

"Cleared to Homestead via left turn direct Miami omni thence via flight planned route. Cross Miami omni at or above 8,000; maintain 23,000 feet."

When Ivory 1 acknowledged the clearance, Howard acknowledged on the radio, "Two copied," then continued the checklist.

"Steering ratio checked."

Ivory 1 was number three to depart behind the two KC-135As, one of which was taking the active runway.

Howard thought to himself, *That's probably our tankers . . . if so, they'll proceed direct to the ARIP and wait for us.*

Approaching runway 5, Bob transmitted, "Before Line-Up Check-list."

"Brakes."

"Set."

"Flight instruments."

Howard and Bob scanned their instrument panel for unusual readings in the attitude indicators, RMI, turn-and-bank, and airspeed. Both pilots responded, "Checked."

"Power controls."

"On. Lights out."

"Flaps."

Howard pulled up and back on the flap handle to the full aft position. In approximately twenty seconds, both pilots respond, "Full down."

"Flight controls."

Bob held his control column in a fixed position as Howard exerted pressure fore and aft to ensure the controls were engaged. Howard moved the column fore and aft to verify freedom of travel, then both pilots transmitted on the intercom, "Engaged."

"Flaperons."

Howard moved the control wheel full left and right while glancing over his shoulders at the wings to verify correct movement of the flaperons, then transmitted, "Checked."

"Trim tabs."

"Set."

"Fuel control panel."

Howard looked to his right and scanned the Fuel Control Panel. Number two fuel selector switch was on TME. The other five fuel selector switches were set on TE.

"Set, lights out."

"Canopy."

"Closed, latched, locked."

"Pins and hooks in place."

"Canopy latch reset."

Howard glanced to his right at the Canopy Latch Reset Panel and verified that the canopy roller lock indicator was in the horizontal, locked position and responded, "Horizontal."

The first tanker began its takeoff roll. The shrill noise and vibration from its four straining Pratt and Whitney turbojet engines penetrated the canopy and Howard's helmet.

His eyes followed the tanker, now halfway down the runway. He stretched his left arm over to the port side of the cockpit to the Oxygen Regulator Panel, flipped the switch to Normal Oxygen, and transmitted, "Switch to normal oxygen."

Leland and Bob made adjustments and replied, "Normal oxygen."

"Circuit breakers."

"Checked."

"Bombsight retractable cover."

Leland responded, "Closed."

Bob transmitted, "Before Line-Up completed."

After the second KC-135A became airborne and began a left turn, a tower controller transmitted, "Wind 090 at 10, altimeter 3016, Ivory 1 and 2 cleared for takeoff."

"Ivory 1, roger. Cleared for takeoff, runway 5."

"Two."

Ivory 1 taxied onto the runway and began their Before Takeoff Checklist. As power was added, black smoke and heat waves swirled from all six engines. Grass at the end of the runway was blown flat to the surface by the full force of the six J47-25A turbojet engines. As the clock approached 2150, the pilot released the brakes, and the B-47B lunged forward, spewing smoke and steam from the water injection mixture. When Ivory 1 was halfway down the runway, Howard moved the throttles forward, then looked left toward final approach for traffic. He continued across the center of the runway and, at a precise time, acquired through years of experience, pressed full right rudder and swung the B-47B around toward the centerline of the runway. When the front wheels were aligned with the centerline, he pressed the top of the rudders with the toe of his shoes and stopped the B-47B.

Bob transmitted, "Before Takeoff Checklist."

"Brakes."

"Holding."

Howard looked down the runway. Ivory 1 was airborne and starting a gentle left turn.

"Compass repeater indicator."

Howard glanced at the compass repeater indicator, which indicated 052, and replied, "Checked."

"Steering ratio selector."

Howard moved the lever with his right hand from TAXI to the TAKEOFF-LAND detent and responded, "Takeoff-land detent."

"Takeoff data."

Howard transmitted, "Go ahead," as he clipped the takeoff and landing data card to his knee-pad.

"Line speed 125 knots, refusal speed 145 knots, take-off speed 162 knots."

"Checked."

"Throttles open."

He slowly pushed the six throttles full forward with his right hand and increased the brake pressure with the toe of his boots. The aircraft vibrated slightly, approaching 100% power, as if it were anxious to fly. Howard's eyes quickly scanned the instrument panel—first to the right for the six tachometers, six fuel pressure gauges, and six EGT gauges; then left to the six oil pressure gauges. All read normal. He thumbed the interphone button and said, "Oil, fuel, EGT okay, 100 percent."

Bob responded, "Alternators and generators checked."

"Nacelles."

"Checked."

"Water injection."

Howard flipped the WATER INJECTION ARM switch to the ON position and looked up as six red lights illuminated on his instrument panel, indicating normal water pressure. He pushed the spring-loaded injection system switch to the START position. After the six red lights shut off, indicating the system was operating, he released the switch and transmitted, "As required."

"Before Takeoff Checklist completed."

Howard scanned the instrument panel one last time. He felt the usual, just-before-takeoff surge of adrenaline in his body.

He removed his toes from the brakes.

Here we go. Slight crosswind. Right aileron down.

CHAPTER SIX

As the aircraft thundered down the runway, Bob observed the needle on the airspeed indicator move to seventy, then transmitted, "Seventy knots."

Howard glanced at his airspeed indicator to cross check its accuracy. The needle was moving through seventy knots also.

Bob continued updating speed information to Howard.

As the line speed checkpoint, located at 2,900 feet, approached, Bob transmitted, "Line speed 125 knots—ready, ready, now."

Howard slowly turned the control wheel left, as less aileron was needed to counteract the cross wind. Bob continued calling out the critical take-off speeds.

"Refusal speed 145 knots—ready, ready, now."

This was a critical time. When the air speed needle passed 145 knots, Howard was committed to take-off. He would not be able to abort the take-off and stop before running off the end of the runway.

"Takeoff speed 162 knots—ready, ready, now."

Howard pulled back slightly on the control column wheel and neutralized the aileron input as the Stratojet gracefully lifted off the runway.

"Gear up," Howard commanded.

Bob pulled the gear leaver out of detent and upward to the up position. Shortly thereafter, the Landing Gear Control Panel tab indicated four up and Bob transmitted, "Four up position indicators."

Howard looked at his landing gear position indicator, which confirmed all four gears were up, then at the airspeed indicator, which had been increasing rapidly. The needle passed through 190 knots. Without the drag from the gear, and the extra thrust from the water injection, the sleek aircraft shot forward like a dart. He pulled back on the control column to increase the rate of climb and stop the airspeed from increasing until the flaps were fully up, then transmitted, "Flaps up."

A Homestead control tower controller observed Ivory 2 lift off. "Ivory 1 and flight contact Miami departure control."

Ivory 1 acknowledged. "Ivory 1, so long." Howard transmitted, "Two," as he switched his radio frequency to 318.4.

The Miami departure radar room was located on the ground floor of the control tower at the Miami International Airport. CAA controllers provided radar services and separation from other aircraft departing, arriving, or over flying their assigned airspace.

While this exchange was ongoing, Bob pulled the flap lever out of the detent position and moved it to the up position, his hand remaining on the lever. He scanned his instruments to verify the position of the gear and flaps, then transmitted, "Gear and flaps." He placed both levers in the OFF position and transmitted, "Levers off."

The co-pilot of Ivory 1 contacted the Miami controller. "Miami departure Ivory 1 and flight climbing through 2,500 for 23,000 feet with the restriction."

"Ivory 1, Miami departure, roger, flash."

"Ivory 1, flashing."

Bob transmitted, "Climb speed."

Howard reduced power on all six engines and transmitted, "Climb power set," as he started a left turn toward the Miami omni.

The controller noted the temporary change in Ivory 1's IFF on his radar display. "Ivory 1, Miami departure, radar contact 5 north of the field."

"Ivory 1, roger."

When Howard completed the left turn to a heading of 360, he noted Ivory 1 at twelve o' clock, approximately two miles. "TO" appeared in the omni tab window. He stopped the left turn at 005 degrees for wind correction.

"Ivory 1, Miami departure, traffic ten o' clock, eight miles eastbound, moderate speed, altitude unknown."

"Ivory 1, looking. Negative joy."

"Two," Howard transmitted, as he scanned the sky for the traffic. "Bob, keep a sharp eye out for that traffic."

"Wilco."

Bob discontinued calling out the checklist and concentrated on the threat. His eagle-like eyes searched the sky for the intruder, knowing it could be thousands of feet above or below their altitude, and no factor. He also recalled how a ground school instructor emphasized that everyone has a small blind spot, even in perfect eyes. This is caused by the entrance of the optic nerve at the back of the eye. The retina has no rods or cones in this small area. An aircraft could hide in this blind spot if the pilot concentrated on looking in only one location. And even a large aircraft could be difficult to acquire at times, particularly if it blends with the background. Equipped with this knowledge, Bob scanned the sky in the vicinity of ten o'clock.

Shortly thereafter, he transmitted over the intercom in a startled voice, "Traffic, a T-bird, eleven o'clock, our altitude."

Howard saw the small, two-seater T-33 at the same instant and turned the B-47B hard to the left in a 60-degree bank.

A moment or so later, after they passed behind and slightly above the silver Air Force trainer, Howard transmitted to Miami departure. "Thanks for the advisory. Was a T-33, our altitude. Passed between me and lead."

"My pleasure to assist you. Glad you missed."

"Same here," Howard responded, as he turned right to get back on course.

Bob continued the checklist. "Water injection."

Howard moved the guard on the ATO panel, pushed the switch to the STOP-and-DRAIN position, then transmitted, "As required."

The six water injection lights illuminated, indicating that the water injection tanks were empty. He placed the Water Injection Switch and the Arm Switch to the OFF position.

As the two blips representing Ivory 1 and 2 neared the edge of the radar scope, the Miami Departure controller keyed his mike and instructed, "Ivory 1 and flight radar service terminated. Contact Miami Center 322.3."

"Ivory 1 switching, and thanks again for the heads-up on the traffic."

"Two."

Both pilots changed their radio to the new frequency.

"Miami Center, Ivory 1, flight of two over the Miami omni at 2159, currently leaving 12,000 climbing to 23,000 feet; estimate Orlando at 2227 Zulu, Tyndall 150 at 125 next."

"Ivory 1, Miami Center, roger. Report leaving 20,000 feet."

"Ivory 1, wilco."

When Howard observed the TO indicator change to FROM, indicating overhead passage of the Miami omni, he turned left to a heading of 345 and rotated the omni course selector knob to the 343 radial for a course direct Orlando omni.

"Crew station check."

Leland responded, "Pressure 305, blinker operating, true airspeed 398 knots."

"Left wing and engine, checked," Bob said. "Pressure 302 pounds, blinker operating. Flight instruments checked, indicated airspeed 358, altitude 14,500 feet, inverter voltages checked, alternator voltages checked, generator loads checked, hydraulic pressure and quantity checked, circuit breakers in, right wing, engines, and empennage checked."

Howard glanced at the rear view mirror and said, "Bob, your aircraft."

Bob grinned, rubbed his gloved hands together in excitement, then gently placed them on the control column wheel and his boots on the rudders. "Roger, my aircraft," he transmitted.

Howard made a note of the time of control transfer on his knee-pad, continued the checklist, and transmitted, "Pressure 303 pounds, blinker operating, oxygen warning indicators checked, flight instruments checked."

Bob transmitted on the aircraft-to-aircraft frequency. "Ivory 1, Ivory 2 is one mile in-trail leaving 17,000. Say indicated air speed."

"Ivory 1, roger. We're also out of 17,000, indicating 340 knots."

Bob and Howard glanced at their indicated airspeed, which was 351 knots. Bob reduced the power slightly to maintain an interval of one mile behind Ivory 1.

Howard noticed a slight movement of the throttles and reflected, *Good thinking . . . stay ahead of the aircraft. He's ready for a command slot.*

Leaving 20,000 feet, the pilot of Ivory 1 transmitted, "Miami Center, Ivory 1 leaving 20,000. Request higher."

"Ivory 1, roger. Contact Miami Center 322.9."

"Ivory 1, roger, switching."

"Two."

"Miami Center, Ivory 1 leaving 21,000 for 23,000 feet."

"Ivory 1, Miami Center, climb and maintain 27,000 feet."

"Ivory 1, roger—27,000."

"Two."

Howard continued the checklist. "Flight instruments checked, indicated airspeed 338 knots, altitude 23,500 feet, engine instruments checked, OAT 20 degrees, power controls on, lights out, fuel panel set as needed, lights out."

"Altimeter set 2992."

Gold 5, a flight of three F86-Ls, checked in with Miami Center as instructed by Jacksonville Center.

"Five."

"Six."

"Seven."

"Miami Center, Gold 5 at 28,000 feet, flight of three F-86s."

"Gold 5, Miami Center, roger."

When Howard overheard Gold 5 check in on the radio at 28,000, he decided to confirm the CAA clearance and instructions with Bob.

"Verify new altitude, 27,000, altimeter set 2992."

Bob responded. "Affirmative, 27,000—2992. Two to go." He turned a knob on the altimeter, adjusting the instrument to 2992.

The Miami CAA Center Air Traffic Controller scanned several handwritten strips of paper that were stuffed into metal holders approximately one inch wide and eight inches long, each strip representing an aircraft. He formulated a picture in his mind of all the aircraft in his sector, concentrating on the two converging flights. He paused, then transmitted, "Ivory 1, traffic a flight of three F-86s over Orlando at 2010, direct Miami, 28,000."

"Ivory 1, copy, negative joy."

"Two looking."

"Ivory 1, report passing the Vero Beach omni 270 radial."

Caught off-guard and not ready for a complex instruction, the pilot of Ivory 1 replied, "Ivory 1, say again," as he prepared to jot down the instructions.

"Ivory 1, report passing the Vero Beach omni 270 radial."

The Ivory 1 pilot noted the instructions on his knee-pad and responded, "Ivory 1, wilco."

"Gold 5, Miami Center traffic a flight of two B-47s over Miami at 2208, direct Orlando climbing to 27,000. Report passing the Vero Beach 270 radial."

"Uh, Miami Gold 5, rog on the traffic. We'll report the fix."

"Tally-ho on the B-47s, eleven o'clock, low."

Leland transmitted on the interphone, "Major Richardson, we departed at 2151 Zulu."

"Rog, 2151." Howard jotted the time in the appropriate box on his knee-pad flight record. "Leland, assume navigational duties at Orlando."

"Wilco, nav at Orlando."

Howard glanced at the altimeter passing 26,000 feet and transmitted to Bob, "Thousand to go."

CHAPTER SEVEN

Bob acknowledged the altitude alert, reduced to cruise power, and trimmed the elevator slightly to climb at 500 feet per minute.

"Heading leaving Orlando will be 261 to ARIP," Leland transmitted.

"Roger, Leland, 261 out of Orlando."

"Miami Center, Ivory 1, tally-ho the three F-86s. We're level 27,000."

"Ivory 1, Miami Center, roger."

Howard sighted the contrails first, then within seconds, the three jet fighters flashed by overhead. An F-86 pilot keyed his mike and transmitted, "Beep, beep," as they passed over Ivory 1.

"Miami, Gold 5 passing Vero Beach 270 radial."

"Gold 5, roger. Expect descent shortly."

"Rog."

"Center, Ivory 1 over the Vero Beach omni 270 radial at 2217 zulu."

"Ivory 1, Miami Center, maintain 27,000 until 2219, climb and maintain 28,000. Time is 2218 Zulu."

"Ivory 1, roger."

"Two."

One minute later, "Miami, Ivory 1 out of 27,000 for 28,000. Request block 28,000 thru 31,000 feet."

Bob glanced at his clock, which was showing 2219, and pulled back slightly on the control column for a slow climb to 28,000.

"Gold 5, Miami descend and maintain 24,000; contact Miami Center on 281.4."

"Gold 5, leaving 28 for 24, switching."

"Six."

"Seven."

"Ivory 1, contact Jacksonville Center on 264.3. They have your request for block altitude."

"Ivory 1, roger."

Howard transmitted, "Two," as he jotted the new frequency on his knee-pad, changed the omni receiver to Orlando, and set in the 342 radial TO Orlando.

"Jacksonville Center, Ivory 1 estimating Orlando omni at 2227, 28,000 feet; Tyndall 150 at 125 next, which is our ARIP."

"Ivory 1, Jacksonville Center, roger."

"Jacksonville, after Orlando, request block altitude for air refueling with Shell 7 and 8."

"Ivory 1, roger. Have your request."

In the meantime, Leland was busy setting up his equipment and computing their groundspeed and headings using the forecast upper winds. In preparation for the air refueling, he turned the rendezvous radar Master Power ON. While the radar unit was warming up, he removed the periscopic sextant from its case and attached it to the overhead mount. Afterwards, he sat the radar receiver standby switch to Standby, flipped the Transmitter and Receiver switches to the prearranged mode 4, turned the receiver standby switch to ON, and adjusted the gain. Pressing his face against the rubber viewing-hood surrounding the radar display, he observed an IFF return at ten o'clock, 175 nautical miles, which he believed to be Shell 7, their tanker.

Leland transmitted on the interphone, "Have Shell 7 flash."

Howard dialed in the pre-arranged UHF refueling frequency, and transmitted on the aircraft-to-aircraft radio, "Shell 7, Ivory 2."

After a slight pause, they heard, "Ivory 2, Shell 7, go ahead."

"Shell 7, flash."

"Shell 7, flashing."

When the pilot of Shell 7 engaged the IFF, a unique code train appeared on Leland's radar display, positively identifying Shell 7 from all other aircraft. Leland transmitted on the interphone, "Radar, contact Shell 7 at ten o'clock and 172 miles."

"Good job, Leland," Howard transmitted. "Ivory 1, Shell 7 is in radar and radio contact."

"Ivory 2, roger, standby."

"Jacksonville Center, Ivory 1 over Orlando at 2227, 28,000 feet, estimating ARIP Tyndall 150 at 125 at 2244 Zulu, New Orleans 180 at 123 next."

"Ivory 1, roger."

The Jacksonville controller forwarded Ivory 1's request to the New Orleans Oceanic controller responsible for the airspace in which the refueling was scheduled to take place and released control to the New Orleans Oceanic controller for block altitude 28,000 through 31,000 feet.

"Ivory 1, contact New Orleans Oceanic on 6567 kilocycles. They have your request."

"Ivory 1, roger, switching 6567."

"Two."

"New Orleans Oceanic, Ivory 1 at 28,000."

"Ivory 1, New Orleans Oceanic, roger. Standby. Shell 8, advise when accepting MARSA with Ivory 1."

"New Orleans Oceanic, Shell 8 is accepting MARSA now."

"Shell 8, roger. You're cleared to conduct air refueling with Ivory 1. Maintain flight level 280 through 310."

"Shell 8, roger. Cleared to tank 28 thru 31."

"Ivory 1, New Orleans Oceanic, maintain flight level 280 through flight level 310. Cleared to tanker frequency."

"Ivory 1, roger, switching."

"Two."

Ivory 1 transmitted to Ivory 2 on the aircraft-to-aircraft refueling frequency, "Ivory 2, climb to angels 30. Ivory 1 will remain at angels 28, over."

"Ivory 2, roger. Verify if Shell 7 is level at angels 31."

"That's affirmative. Shell 7 at angels 31; Shell 8 at angels 29."

"Roger, Ivory 2 climbing to angels 30."

"Ivory 1 is changing to pre-arranged refueling frequency."

"Rog, talk to you after re-fuel."

"I've got the controls, Bob," Howard transmitted. "Prepare for air-refueling."

"Roger, your aircraft."

"Rog, my aircraft."

"Farther left to heading 255," Leland transmitted.

"Roger, left to 255. Where's Shell 7?"

Leland squinted as he studied his radar set and replied, "Shell 7 is twelve o'clock, 72 miles."

Howard transmitted, "Shell 7, Ivory 2 is 72 miles east, climbing to angels 30; estimating ARIP at 2244, over."

"Ivory 2, Shell 7, roger."

"Ready for Air Refueling Checklist," Bob transmitted.

"Go ahead."

"Rendezvous equipment."

Leland transmitted, "On."

"Altimeter 2992."

All three crew members verified 2992 in the altimeter box, then responded, "Set."

"Gross weight 145,000, contact indicated air speed 220."

"Slipway heat."

"On."

"ESP switch on."

"On."

"Directional damper."

"As required."

"Trim, seats, and pedals."

"Adjusted."

"Fuel panel."

"Set."

"Master refuel switch."

Howard moved his Master Refuel switch located on the Fuel Control Panel from NORMAL to REFUEL. This energized the refueling valve switches, fuel quantity gauges, and panel lights on Bob's refueling panel.

"Refuel."

"Refueling panel lights."

"Tested."

"Fuel quantity indicators."

"Checked."

"Tanks to be refueled."

"Valves open on forward main, center main, and aft main tanks. All other valves closed."

"Co2 selector."

"As required."

"Air refueling selector switch."

"Normal."

"Air refueling valve lever."

"Open."

"Circuit breakers."

"Checked."

"Air refueling lights."

"On."

"Radio."

Howard and Bob transmitted, "Command," as they switched their radios to command.

"Periscopic sextant."

Leland transmitted, "Removed."

"Automatic pilot."

"Off."

"Flaps."

Howard observed the indicated air speed, lowered the flaps to 10 degrees, and responded, "Set, ten degrees."

"No smoking."

All three crew members transmitted, "No smoking."

"Slipway door."

"Open."

Howard transmitted to Leland, "Say position of Shell 7."

"Shell 7 is twelve o'clock, 21 miles."

"Shell 7, Ivory 2 is 21 east at angels 30, slowing to 220 indicated. Say angels."

"Shell 7 is turning eastbound at angels 31."

Howard placed his right hand over his visor to shield the sun. "Shell 7, roger. Negative tally, lots of glare from the setting sun."

"Leland, keep me advised of Shell 7's position."

"Roger that. Shell 7 is twelve o'clock, eleven miles."

"Shell 7, Ivory 2 is eleven east."

"Ivory 2, roger. Tally-ho two B-47s. We're indicating 220, starting our turn westbound."

Howard squinted as he searched for the tanker, then transmitted, "Shell 7, roger, tally-ho."

"Unnecessary electrical equipment."

Howard turned off his omni and radio compass. Bob turned off the liaison radio and fire control equipment. Leland turned off the rendezvous radar. As each crew member turned off their equipment, they transmitted, "Off."

"Fuel panel."

"Rechecked."

Air refueling lights."

"Adjusted."

Howard glanced at the indicated air speed showing 228, then transmitted, "Flaps 20 degrees."

"Twenty degrees and set."

"Checklist complete. Ready for contact."

Bob transmitted to Shell 7, "Ivory 2, ready for contact."

CHAPTER EIGHT

oward began a slow ascent maintaining a safe distance behind his tanker, leveled off approximately 200 feet below the KC-135A. The boom operator lowered and partially extended the boom, then transmitted in a friendly southern drawl, "Good evening, Ivory 2, you're looking good. Clean your windshield, check your oil if I could. Got both regular and unleaded. Come on up, but keep her steady."

Howard adjusted the elevator trim tab and began a very slow climb. "He's something else," he muttered to himself. "Must be bored, or ready for discharge. Hope this clown knows what he's doing."

Howard transmitted without comment, "Ready for pre-contact."

Then suddenly, as if a switch had been thrown, the boom operator's voice changed. His instructions were crisp and explicit. All business. "Two degrees port. Thirty feet to go. Increase altitude slightly . . . forward 15." The rays of the setting sun reflected off the windshield of Ivory 2 into the eyes of the boom operator. He pulled his visor down over his eyes, concentrating on the position of Ivory 2 and his probe. Howard increased the throttles a minuscule, keeping his eyes focused on the nozzle. The boom operator appeared in his peripheral vision as he inched the Stratojet closer and closer. One small mistake could result in a collision between the two aircraft. Fortunately, the air was smooth.

Howard moved the throttles ever so slightly, almost imperceptibly, fine-tuning the ailerons, elevator, and rudder as if they were a musical instrument.

"Ten feet to go, on altitude, reduce throttles just a tad . . . perfect."

The boom operator extended the probe farther and guided it straight into the receptacle. "Clunk." Bob glanced at his air refueling panel to verify that the Contact-Made light had illuminated and the Ready-for-Contact light had extinguished, then transmitted, "Receiver contact made."

"New Orleans Oceanic, Shell 7 ARIP at 2244 with Ivory 2 in tow."

"Shell 7, New Orleans, roger."

Howard glanced up at the Pilot Director Light System located on the belly of the KC-135A. A green light glowed, which meant he was in a nominal position to continue refueling.

All right, Richardson, steady as she goes. Let's do this right the first time.

Fuel began flowing at a high rate into the forward main tank, which Bob had selected. Howard began his balancing act by adding power to compensate for the extra weight as fuel gushed into the tank. The tanker pilot compensated for the lost weight. When the fuel quantity gauge read 19,000 pounds, Bob transmitted to the boom operator, "Reduce pressure to 35 PSI."

"Roger, 35 PSI."

When the fuel quantity gauge neared the full mark of 20,000 pounds, Bob flipped on the Refueling Valve Switch for the rear main tank, closed the valve for the forward main tank, and instructed the boom operator to return to normal pressure.

Air refueling required a detailed knowledge of the fuel system. Safety valves were built-in to prevent loading excessive fuel into a tank. However, the preferred and safest procedure was to carefully regulate the fuel flow so that the safety valves were not relied upon. When the rear main was nearly full, he flipped the switch and closed the valve, then refueled the center main tank. He thumbed the disconnect switch on the control column as he transmitted, "Receiver disconnect."

Howard's windscreen wipers activated automatically as the disconnect occurred. He returned the boom operator's salute, reduced power to increase separation from Shell 7, and started a descent to angels 30.

As the boom operator retracted the boom, he transmitted, "I'll send the bill by mail. Y'all have a safe mission."

Howard smiled and responded, "Good job. See ya next trip."

Bob began the Post-refueling Checklist.

"Tanker clear."

"Clear."

"Slipway door."

"Closed."

"Flaps."

"Up."

"All refueling switches."

"Off."

"Air refueling selector switch."

"Off."

"Air refueling valve lever."

"Closed."

"Air refueling lights."

"Off."

"Master refuel switch."

"Normal."

"Fuel gage control."

"Pilot."

"Altimeters."

All crew members replied, "Set 2992."

"ESP switch."

"Off."

"Checklist complete."

Fuel in the two external drop tanks would be burnt first. In case of an emergency, it might become necessary to jettison the tanks. It would be better if they were empty. Howard switched all six Fuel Selector switches to TME, turned the Auxiliary-Fuel-to-Engine toggle switch to the Valve-Open position, and turned the boost pumps on for both wing tanks. In this configuration, a shut-off valve was open, allowing fuel to flow from the external drop tanks directly to the engine manifolds. He made a notation of the time on his knee-pad and announced on the interphone, "Using external fuel tanks."

He stretched to his left in order to reach the Position Light Panel and turned the navigation lights on in the flashing mode, dome light on in red, then transmitted, "Position and navigation lights on."

"Resume navigation responsibility," he transmitted to Leland.

"Roger that. Estimate egress fix at New Orleans 180 at 123 at 2344 Zulu."

Howard glanced at the cockpit clock as the sun sank below the horizon.

Nine minutes to go. Wonder if Ivory 1 is still tanking . . . keep the speed at 220 til they finish.

Howard stretched his left arm to reach the Oxygen Regulator Panel, flipped the Pressure Demand Oxygen Regulator switch to the OFF position, and then transmitted over the interphone, "Removing oxygen mask." Shortly thereafter, Bob and Leland reported removing their oxygen masks. The mask remained attached to the helmet for immediate use in case of decompression or other emergency.

Bob grabbed his Seat Tilt and Rotation handle with his right hand and rotated the seat 180 degrees. "Guns to warm-up and standby," he transmitted, before turning the selector switch on the turret control panel to WARM-UP and noting the current time. After the required ten minutes for warm-up expired, STANDBY was selected for an additional twenty minutes to preheat the guns, feeder, and system heaters. He turned the Selector switch to the OPERATE position and adjusted the IF Gain, scope Illumination, Intensity, and the Range Selector switch to 8,000 yards. Last, the Turret Control panel altitude knobs were turned to 30,000 feet, the outside temperature to minus 35, and a true airspeed of 425 knots. The guns were ready for action. Since actual firing would not occur, Bob rechecked to ensure the Gun Safety Switch was set on the SAFE position, then announced, "Guns operational, safety switch on."

Howard looked right and left searching for Ivory 1. When he turned to full left, he glimpsed two aircraft in the twilight at eight o'clock and low, apparently refueling.

Running late. Probably had trouble hooking up.

Leland retrieved the periscopic sextant and mounted it overhead his seat in the top of the fuselage in preparation for celestial navigation.

Ivory 1 called on the aircraft-to-aircraft frequency, "Ivory 2, you up?"

Howard looked to his left and saw Ivory 1 at nine o'clock low, then transmitted, "Ivory 1, affirmative. Have visual contact. What took you so long?"

"Valve problem, but it finally decided to function. Let's switch to New Orleans Oceanic on 6567."

"Roger, 6567kc, switching."

"Two."

CHAPTER NINE

"**N**ew Orleans Oceanic, Ivory 1 estimating egress at 2345, in block flight level 28 through 31, terminate air refueling and MARSA. Ivory 1 is currently VFR conditions on top, request VFR conditions on top."

"Ivory 1, New Orleans Oceanic, roger. Maintain VFR conditions on top."

"Ivory 1, wilco. Altitude will be 28.5."

Howard transmitted, "Two," as he reduced power and started descent to 28,500 feet, keeping Ivory 1 in sight.

"At egress, turn right heading 339," Leland transmitted.

"Roger, 339 at egress."

When Howard estimated he was a mile behind Ivory 1, he increased the throttle setting until the indicated speed read 390 knots, then transmitted, "Ivory 2 at angels 28.5; indicated air speed 390."

Howard glanced at his watch, which indicated 2342. *Lead should start a right turn shortly.*

He thumbed the interphone and transmitted, "Bob, it's your aircraft. Any questions?"

"Negative questions. I have the aircraft."

Howard noted the time on his knee-pad, unfolded his navigational chart, and located the frequency of the New Orleans omni. He changed the frequency and adjusted the course selector knob to 360 degrees. A "TO" indication appeared in the tab window confirming that they were south of the New Orleans omni.

Thermos bottles and drinking cups were stowed on the left side of the co-pilot position, out of the pilot's reach. Howard glanced in his rear view mirror at Bob and transmitted, "Bob, hand me my thermos and a cup, please."

Bob retrieved the thermos and cup, leaned forward, and passed them to Howard.

He opened his thermos, poured a half cup, securely tightened the lid, and gave it back to Bob. "Thanks, Bob," he said, smiling. "As always, you are welcome to try some of the best coffee in Florida."

"Thank you, sir. I'll have some later tonight."

Howard unzipped his leather jacket and retrieved an envelope containing a recent family photograph from his flight suit. He pulled the tape back and attached the photograph onto the center of the control column. He stared at his favorite portrait of the family, which had been taken at the First Baptist Church of Homestead for the membership yearbook. When the photograph was made, he had procrastinated on whether to wear his uniform or a civilian suit. At the last moment, his family strongly encouraged him to wear his uniform for the portrait and now, on reflection, he was pleased with that decision. He smiled as he gazed at the photograph.

A fine looking family if I do say so myself. Kids and Vivian look great. I'm really fortunate.

He sipped the steaming coffee and smiled. *Bet they're watching their favorite TV show or playing a game. I'll be there tomorrow night. Maybe go out to eat and take in a family movie . . . maybe a drive-in movie. That'd be nice while the weather is cool and the mosquitoes are at bay. However, may not be a good idea on a school night . . .*

He unzipped a pocket on his flight suit, pulling out a half-empty pack of Lucky Strikes and a Zippo lighter with the image of a B-47B on one side and Strategic Air Command engraved on the opposite side. He turned the pack sideways, thumped the bottom with his index finger, and removed a cigarette. Placing it in his mouth, he replaced the pack. Almost unconsciously, he flipped the Zippo lid backward and spun the wheel with his thumb while scanning the flight instruments. When the Zippo ignited, he moved the blaze to the cigarette, sucking deeply. The end of the cigarette turned bright orange. He clicked the lid closed and replaced the Zippo in his flight suit pocket, exhaling smoke through his nostrils. As he reached for the coffee cup, he coughed deeply, almost spilling some of it.

Should listen to the flight surgeon's advice and quit this nasty habit, he thought. *Been smoking since I was . . . eleven years old. Even the Boy*

Scouts wouldn't accept me until I quit. Started again soon afterwards. Would make Vivian very happy . . . She never complains, but I know she greatly dislikes the ashes, burnt clothing, burnt car seats . . . and the noxious smell.

When Howard's omni needle crossed the 358 bearing to New Orleans, Ivory 1 began a right turn and transmitted, "New Orleans Oceanic, Ivory 1, progress report."

There was a slight pause, then, "Ivory 1, New Orleans, go ahead."

"Ivory 1 over New Orleans 180 at 123 at 2344 Zulu, IFR, VFR conditions on top at flight level 28.5. Estimating Mc Comb omni 266 at 042 at 0011; Little Rock 275 at 008 next."

"Ivory 1, New Orleans Oceanic, roger. Contact New Orleans Center 363.2 at 0005."

"Ivory 1, roger, 363 decimal 2."

Howard jotted down the instructions onto his knee-pad and acknowledged, "Two."

Bob began a coordinated right turn and rolled out on a heading of 339.

Bob's doing a great job. As soon as I can arrange it, I want to put him up here in the pilot seat . . . I'll instruct him from the co-pilot seat. That way he can get the real feel of the aircraft. Flying from the rear seat is good training, but it's not the same as being up here in the aircraft commander's seat. He sipped his coffee and took a drag from the Lucky Strike. *Make all the major decisions when you're sitting in this seat. He needs training in several critical areas—air refueling and lobbing the bomb. He's a quick learner . . . won't take a lot of flight time to get him up to speed.*

Ivory 1 transmitted over the aircraft-to-aircraft radio. "Two, let's go to 363.2."

"Two, switching."

"Two."

Howard rolled the half-smoked Lucky Strike back and forth between his gloved index finger and thumb, doused the fire in the control column ash tray, and mused, *That's the first and last one on this mission . . . maybe forever. No more yellow fingers. Good riddance.*

The lights of the Crescent City glistened in the far distance.

He located the Mc Comb omni frequency on his navigational chart, turned the knob to the new frequency, then rotated the course selector knob to 266 degrees.

Ivory 1 checked in on the new frequency. "New Orleans Center, Ivory 1. VFR conditions on top at 28,500. Estimate Mc Comb omni 266 at 043 miles at 0011."

More than five miles below, on the second floor of the New Orleans Lakefront Airport Terminal Building, a young CAA controller cupped his hand over his ear and pressed on his headset to blot out noise as the first transmission from Ivory 1 crackled. Pulling his two-colored pencil out of his shirt pocket holder, he slid off his elevated chair, ready to write. When Ivory 1 transmitted, "Estimate Mc Comb omni . . ." the controller's eyes focused first on the portion of the board in which the Mc Comb strip was located or "posted," then for a strip containing the call sign, Ivory 1. When he located the strip that was sequenced between eleven others, he entered a checkmark by the altitude, indicating to the other controllers that Ivory 1 was on frequency, VFR-on-top at 28,500 feet. It was not necessary for him to enter the estimated time or altitude on the strip because the Oceanic Controller had forwarded this information to the Mc Comb controller shortly after Ivory 1 reported over the New Orleans fix.

The controller, located in the Air Route Traffic Control Center, or commonly called "Center" in aviation circles, keyed his mike and transmitted, "Ivory 1, New Orleans Center, roger," then scanned the board to determine whether any traffic information should be issued to Ivory 1. Because Ivory 1 was operating VFR on top, separation from other aircraft was not provided by the CAA controller, but traffic information would be issued, workload permitting.

Like all the other controllers, he wore the unofficial uniform of black shoes, dark trousers, and a white shirt with matching tie, topped off with a flat-top haircut. The Control Room was busy, with controllers receiving incoming calls, recording data on the strips, and scanning for aircraft conflicts. When aircraft report over compulsory reporting points, usually navigational aids, and the time is different from the Center estimated time, a quick calculation is made with an E6-B computer to determine the new groundspeed. The controller determines a revised estimate for the next checkpoint and forwards the revised estimate and groundspeed to the downstream controller.

Assistant controllers prepared hand-written strips for flight plans received from Air Carrier Operations, CAA Flight Service Stations, and adjacent Centers. Controllers received and forwarded flight data to controllers within the New Orleans Center as well as adjacent Centers located at Atlanta, Jacksonville, Memphis, Fort Worth, and San Antonio. The Oceanic Controllers are responsible for the majority of airspace overlying the Gulf of Mexico. In this endeavor, they coordinate with several Central American countries and Cuba. Some incoming calls from adjacent centers were initiated through a blaring speaker, and some outgoing calls were initiated by dialing an antiquated rotary dial phone that made a clicking sound when each number was dialed. The process of re-sequencing the metal strip holders when time revisions were made and when new strips were delivered by the assistant controllers added to the noise level.

The New Orleans Center had recently opened four new sectors known as "High Altitude" sectors in preparation for the control of civil jets and to take pressure off of the low latitude sectors. Due to several recent mid-air collisions and numerous near misses, the number of aircraft flying on an IFR clearance, regardless of the weather conditions, had dramatically increased over the past year. Consequently, the CAA split the airspace vertically at and above 24,000 feet. The "low-altitude" sectors retained the airspace at and below 23,000 feet, except for airspace released to control towers for terminal operations. The CAA was finally awakening to new technology. The recently installed VHF and UHF radio frequencies for the high-altitude sectors were located at Mobile, Alabama, and Alexandra, Louisiana. Telephone lines connected the radio sites to the Center. They provided complete radio coverage within the high-altitude sectors.

Previously, the Center had been without radios, except for the Oceanic Control. Aircraft made position reports to either a CAA Flight Service Station or to an Air Carrier operations center, who in turn forwarded the information to the Centers via telephone—the same awkward procedure used since Centers were invented in 1935. Having direct radio contact with pilots was safer because it eliminated the "time-lag" problem when information was relayed through another company or CAA facility. A spin-off was improved controller efficiency. Unfortunately, it would be several years before the low altitude sectors would be provided with their own frequencies.

Because of the desperate need for more controllers, the CAA Academy at Oklahoma City operated at full capacity, utilizing two shifts in their effort to train new recruits in the basics of air traffic control. Those who graduated were sent to CAA facilities that were critically short of controllers. At the CAA facility, they received additional training to become assistant controllers, and later, more formal and on-the-job training to certify as a controller.

Leland transmitted to Bob, "Turn left to heading 334."

"Roger, left to heading 334."

So far, everything's been executed as planned, Howard thought. *That was a smooth tank. Boom operator was competent once he got into it. Voice sounds familiar . . . I believe that's the joker that rattled me last year when I tanked with a KC-97. Initially thought it was a shriveled up, really old airman. The more I stared, the more confused I became. What a nose. Hard to believe.*

The boom operator had brought his well-trained dog with him, put a helmet on the dog, and set him in the operator's seat. The 97 crew laughed their guts out listening to Howard trying to be diplomatic with a dog. That one bounced around the base for quite some time. He had taken lots of good-natured ribbing. One of their favorites was, "When he finished filling your tanks, did he cock his leg and clean your windshield?"

Never did hear if he was disciplined. Doubt if he was because the entire crew was involved. Hope not. He did a professional tank that day just as he did today.

"New Orleans, Ivory 1 position report."

"Ivory 1, go ahead."

"Roger, Center. Ivory 1 progressed over Mc Comb 266 radial at 040 miles at 0012, VFR conditions on top at 28,500 feet; estimate Little Rock 275 at 005 at 0043. Butler radials next."

"Ivory 1, roger. Contact Memphis Center 301.4."

"Ivory 1, roger, switching."

"Two."

One minute later, "Memphis Center, Ivory 1 VFR conditions on top at 28,500; estimate Little Rock 275 at 005 at 0043 Zulu."

"Ivory 1, Memphis Center, roger."

CHAPTER TEN

The lights of Jackson Mississippi glowed at Howard's two o'clock position. Farther northeast loomed Louisville, his hometown. Memories begin to flood through his head.

Wonder how the family's doing tonight? Should call next weekend and touch base with Mom and Dad. They're doing great but not getting any younger. Wonder when Dad will retire and turn his practice over to David? He really enjoys being a physician, helping others . . . Probably continue working . . . and why not?

Chop and contrails from Ivory 1 is . . . irritating.

"Bob, suggest you move a few hundred yards starboard," Howard transmitted, "enough to clear leads wake turbulence and contrails."

"Wilco. Will be a bit smoother ride."

"Affirmative. Should be."

Howard continued reminiscing. *A few months ago, Uncle started construction of a Naval Air Station at Meridian. Columbus and Green-ville Air Force Bases and the Naval Station at Meridian sure helps prop up the local economy. And the National Guard helps, too . . . Hard to imagine what it would be like without them.*

"Leland, when you get an extra minute, give me an estimate for the Eastern ADIZ penetration."

"Yes sir, Major. I've already calculated that time. Stand by one . . . I estimate penetration eleven minutes after Little Rock radials, or 0053."

That's pretty darn good, Howard thought. *Thinking ahead. Good man.* He jotted down the time.

"Thanks, Leland. What body are you using for the cel-nav?"

"Sirius. Getting ready to shoot the moon. She's a beauty tonight."

Howard looked up at the full moon, with some of its features clearly visible. It seemed so close that he could reach out and touch it.

"Couldn't agree more. Bob, after we pass Little Rock, keep a sharp eye out for fighters."

"Roger that, Major. You authorizing evasive maneuvers?"

"Unfortunately, we're not authorized to take evasive action. Wish we could. We'll probably get hammered as we get closer to Grand Forks Air Force Base. If so, suggest you practice some with the A-5 guns."

"Roger that."

Howard transmitted in a halfway joking manner, "And Bob, don't forget to keep the safety switch on. Don't want to accidentally shoot down a comrade."

"Roger that. Would spoil everybody's day. Especially mine."

"You got it."

Howard refreshed his coffee, scanned the fuel control panel, and mused, *Burned off enough fuel for a higher altitude . . . Remember to switch to the rear main tank at approximately 0135 Zulu.* He made a note on his knee-pad to make the switch.

"Memphis Center, Ivory 1 progress report."

"Ivory 1, Memphis Center, go ahead."

"Memphis Center, Ivory 1 over Little Rock radials at 0041, IFR, VFR on top at 28,500 feet; estimate Butler 071 at 040 at 0114, Des Moines radials next. At approximately 0055, we will climb to 32,000 feet."

"Ivory 1, roger. Contact Kansas City Center on 381.4 at 0100."

"Ivory 1, roger. Good evening."

"Adios."

At 0055, Ivory 1 transmitted on the aircraft-to-aircraft frequency, "Ivory 1 and flight climb to angels 32, now."

"Two."

Bob added power and adjusted the elevator trim for a slightly nose high attitude and started climbing to 32,000 feet.

At 0100 Zulu, Ivory 1 checked in on the new frequency. "Kansas City Center, Ivory 1 climbing to 32,000 feet."

Ivory 1, Kansas City, roger. Report reaching 32,000."

"Ivory 1, ro—"

"Two, traffic at two o'clock, high."

His head jerked up from the Pilot Flight Progress Chart and Log, his eyes focused as they searched the starry sky.

"No joy . . . uh, tally-ho, one o'clock high."

"Center, Ivory 1 has westbound traffic at one o'clock about two miles. Have anything on him?"

"Ivory 1, standby."

Seconds later, Center transmitted in a somewhat unsettled voice, "Ivory 1, that's probably a B-52 westbound at 35,000 feet, over."

"Ivory 1, roger. Concur. We're level at 32,000 and a westbound B-52 is passing at twelve o'clock. Thanks."

"Ivory 1, roger. Center normally doesn't issue traffic information if 3,000 feet or greater vertical separation exists."

"Roger that. But it's kinda hard to determine the altitude of the other aircraft, especially at night."

"Ivory 1, this is Beagle 43, had you in sight. Where ya based?"

"Homestead. And you?"

"Castle."

"Beagle, uh 43, roger that. You put out quite a contrail with that beast . . . got bumped around when we went through your wake."

"Rog . . . Hope we didn't spill your soup. Have a good flight."

"Same to ya."

At that very instant, 600 nautical miles east-southeast, at Charleston, South Carolina Air Force Base, several young fighter pilots entered the hanger where a row of F-86L fighters were neatly parked at the 444th Fighter Interceptor Squadron. They chatted as they made their way up a set of stairs to the alert room and struck up a conversation with the other arriving pilots and those being relieved. Normally there would be a briefing by the outgoing flight commander as well as the incoming flight commander while both alert crews were present. If an active scramble were initiated before the incoming crew was fully briefed, had gathered their gear, and preflighted their aircraft, the on-duty crew would respond. But this was anything but routine alert duty. Four additional pilots, crew chiefs, and other airmen, as needed, had been called in for extra alert duty.

The Second Air Force, subordinate to CINCSAC, issued Operation Order 300-57 directing the 19th Bomb Wing, Homestead Air Force Base, to conduct a Uniform Simulated Combat Mission (USCM) dubbed Southern Belle. This mission consisted of approximately twenty B-47Bs and several KC-135A tanker aircraft. This order stated that fighter attacks would not be made on Southern Belle B-47Bs south of the simulated bomb drop at Radford, Virginia. On 29 January 1958, CINCSAC forwarded secret message DOOPO 1175 to CINCNORAD. This message gave authority to CINCNORAD to make fighter intercepts against Southern Belle B-47Bs without any restrictions as to location, which was contrary to the 2nd Air Force order. Whether or not the 2nd Air Force, located at Barksdale Air Force Base, received a copy of this message is unknown. CINCNORAD forwarded this information to the 35th Air Division, who subsequently published 35th Air Division Operations Order 1-58 authorizing fighter intercepts to be made against Southern Belle B-47Bs anywhere within the 35th Air Division area of responsibility, which encompassed the southeast United States.

Due to the USCM mission and two recent pilot fatalities from the 444th, the Commanding Officer, Lieutenant Colonel Sam C. Johnson Jr., decided to personally brief the pilots, aircraft crew chiefs, and maintenance personnel concerning safety. As Johnson entered the small briefing room, Captain J. H. Weber Jr. called the room to attention. Some of the lower ranking enlisted airmen were standing in the back of the room because of inadequate seating for such a large group.

Johnson strode quickly to the podium, a concerned look on his face.

"At ease, gentlemen." He paused, turned his head slowly, surveying the room. "I'll make this quick and straight to the point. I realize some of you have been on duty for twelve hours and want to go home or whatever. Safety, safety, safety. We must all keep safety in mind at all times. Above everything else. It's imperative that we do so. I consider the two recent accidents as unacceptable both in terms of human and equipment loss. Three aircraft lost in one day. The tragedy of losing two of our good pilots, whom I consider part of my military family, weighs heavily upon me." Johnson's voice quavered as his emotions almost overcame him. He swallowed, cleared his throat, and continued.

"Fortunately, First Lieutenant Raymond Bronk survived the mid-air collision and is expected to be released from the Naval hospital tomorrow. I spoke with him briefly this afternoon. I didn't dwell too much on the accident. Perhaps he can shed more light on why the collision occurred after he is released. Both aircraft, or parts thereof, have been recovered and will help us in the accident investigation process. The other accident was apparently caused by engine flameout shortly after becoming airborne, with not enough room to stop the aircraft before exiting the runway. At this point, we don't know the cause of the failure, but we usually start at maintenance procedures. So we have two areas of concern—two areas for probable improvement. Perhaps a different attitude toward safety is needed. Maintenance and flight operations are prime candidates for improvement. So, I challenge every man in this room to set an example for each other. Think carefully about each and every thing you do. Challenge anything that doesn't seem right. If not performed correctly, by the book, it could result in another tragic accident. We are in charge of and are responsible for the most sophisticated, complex, and costly fighters ever built. Do your part to save lives and aircraft. Thank you, and fly safely."

Captain Weber called the room to attention until the CO exited, then said, "At ease, gentlemen. You heard what the boss said. He's very concerned, as well he should be. And so am I. Tonight's operation must be carried out with great diligence. SAC has put twenty B-47s in the air. They're operating out of Homestead on a USCM mission. How many of these aircraft, if any, will fly through our area of jurisdiction is unknown. Since additional personnel have been put on duty, this suggests that at least some of these flights will involve us. I have kept in touch with weather, and they're predicting clear skies, a full moon, and quite cold temperatures for Charleston. That's all I have, unless you have questions."

A young second lieutenant inquired, "Will the B-47s use evasive maneuvers?"

"Evasive maneuvers were not mentioned in the ops order. Those SAC boys might try anything. Could try to outrun you." The room erupted in laughter, a release from the high tension brought on by the two fatal accidents and a tough night ahead. He continued. "The B-47B has a radar warning system in the tail and nose. So if you approach from these directions with your radar on, the system alerts the co-pilot of your presence. The B-47B is also equipped with a gun-laying radar, which is located in the tail section and controls two cannons. If you intercept from the rear, they will most likely know you're there and try to outrun or out-maneuver you."

Another pilot asked, "Do they operate with their anti-collision or navigation lights off?"

Captain Weber shook his head. "Negative. They're supposed to be on. In addition to the standard navigation lights, two lights, one yellow and one white, are located on top of the vertical fin. White position lights are located on the top and bottom of the fuselage. But I want to caution you, these lights are difficult to see until you get close in. This is particularly true on a clear night, with stars and surface lights for a background. The aircraft lights can blend in with these competing lights. Use caution."

"If there are no further questions, I'll turn the briefing over to my relief, Captain Webb."

Captain Webb walked to the podium. "Thank you, Captain Weber. There's not much that I can add to what has already been said about safety. The life you save may be your own. Be careful. Be cautious. Remember the basics, and use your checklist. As you probably noticed entering the hangar, we have eight aircraft on alert duty, plugged in and ready to go. Six of these aircraft, Pug Silver and Pug Gold, are reserved for the USCM. The other two are for active scrambles on unknown bogies. We have the option to convert Pug Silver and Pug Gold to active scramble duty at any time. The scramble order from Hemingway will specify whether it's for USCM training. If we are scrambled for USCM aircraft, Pug Silver will go first and, if necessary, Pug Gold next. Okay men, let's head to the locker room, get your gear, prep your aircraft, and wait for the horn. And above all, fly safely."

CHAPTER ELEVEN

Ivory 1 checked in with Kansas City Center as instructed. "Kansas City Center, Ivory 1. IFR, VFR on top at 32,000; estimate Butler 071 radial at forty miles at 0112 Zulu."

"Ivory 1, Kansas City Center, roger."

Howard topped off his coffee and retrieved a ham and cheese sandwich from his flight lunch. As he ate, he stretched and moved his legs around to improve blood circulation. He contemplated on the earlier encounter with the T-33 and B-52. *That B-52 could have been at our altitude if they had been operating VFR on top. It's hard to see an aircraft's lights, even a large one, when blended against the background of a starry night. And that T-Bird blended in with the earth's surface. Just came out of nowhere. Good thing Homestead gave us a heads up on that one. I should write a letter to that controller's boss for a possible save. A few years ago, when I first started flying jets, we didn't worry much about traffic . . . except when departing and arriving near the air bases. At the rate Uncle's cranking out jet aircraft, the sky is becoming crowded up here.*

Leland's voice crackled in Howard's helmet. "Bob, change course—turn right to a heading of 340."

"Roger, right to 340."

Howard observed the course change on his RMI and the N-1 compass. The azimuth card turned and stopped exactly on 340.

Smooth, coordinated turn. Good job, Bob.

He swallowed the last of his sandwich, scanned the instruments, and resumed his deep thinking of what the future might be like.

There is concern, and disagreement, within the Pentagon and CAA on how the civil jets will . . . fit into the system. . . . When we visited the

Miami Center, the briefer said none of the Centers currently have radar and only a handful of the larger civilian fields, like Miami, have terminal radar. I was shocked when we entered the Control Room. In an old rented building. Controllers stretching headset cords across the room, yelling info at each other. Those strips . . . everywhere. Handwritten scribbles all over them. Some written in red. They tried to explain what some of the controllers and coordinators were doing. Assured us everything was under control. It looked like mad chaos—mass confusion . . . bedlam. I wasn't convinced, but it sounds perfectly normal from this end.

How the CAA controllers keep aircraft separated using those handwritten slips of paper they call strips is still a mystery to me. Developing new long-range radars and putting them into service will probably take years. Then there will be the massive program of training Center controllers in a new technology . . . I don't know how it'll work out. Probably take another mid-air collision like the one over the Grand Canyon to shake things up. Hope not . . . but on the other hand, I don't want to lose my freedom of flying . . . too much interference from ground control could adversely affect our daily training . . . be fatal to our defensive posture. It's probably coming, like it or not. Boeing has already flown their four-engine civilian jet, and Douglas is not far behind with their jet. In a year or so, they'll be up here with us, competing for airspace.

Ivory1 reported over the Butler fix to Kansas City Center, estimated Des Moines omni 235 radial at 059 miles at 0134 and Sioux Falls radials next.

I'll switch to the aft auxiliary tank at Des Moines. Bob's keeping a good interval behind Ivory 1. Staying on altitude and heading . . . like the instruments are glued in place. Probably getting tired of hand flying, but he can't learn much on auto-pilot. I'll relieve him if we ever get some interceptors so he can practice with his guns. He glanced at his rear-view mirror to observe Bob and transmitted, "How's things going, Bob?"

"Good, as far as I know. Enjoying every minute. So far no fighters."

"Yeah, kinda makes you wonder if they know we're up here and just waiting to pounce on us later . . . surprise us. Could be part of the old cat-and-mouse game. I really expected some action when we entered the ADIZ. Bob, if you need a break, just let me know."

"Sure will, Major. Thanks."

"Leland, you doing okay down there? Temperature need adjusting?"

"Just fine. Very comfortable. Nice, smooth ride like tonight sure helps on these long flights. Especially a big guy like me. Just took another star shot. According to my calculations, we're right on course, on time."

"Must be. We're maintaining the same track as Ivory 1. Leland, when we approach the target later tonight, Bob will make a celestial shot if you need some help."

"Okay, thanks. I'll keep that in mind. I'll mainly use radar navigation, but a backup is reassuring. Thanks, Major. For now, I'm having something to eat."

"Ham and cheese was good. Crisp lettuce for a change."

"Sounds good. Haven't eaten since breakfast. Trying to keep the pounds at a reasonable number."

"Know what you mean."

Howard scanned the instrument panel, then checked the wing tank quantity indicators on the Fuel Control Panel, which confirmed that both tanks were almost exhausted. He glanced at his watch, which indicated 0130 Zulu, thumbed the interphone switch, and transmitted, "Switching from wing tanks to aft auxiliary." He flipped the Boost Toggle Switch to the ON position for the aft auxiliary fuel tank and made a note of the time on his knee-pad. About ten minutes later, he turned the drop tank boost pump switches to OFF when the No-Flow warning lights illuminated, indicating the tanks were empty. This was confirmed by the Quantity Indicators showing empty. He calculated the fuel burn at angels 32, using the current power setting as 165 pounds per minute. At that rate, the aft tank would last fifty minutes. Using fuel from the proper tanks was critical in order to maintain the center of gravity. He made a note on his knee-pad to switch to the bomb bay tank not later than 0220, and transmitted, "Aft aux tank should expire at 0220 at the current burn rate of 165 pounds per minute."

Ivory 1 reported over the Sioux Falls omni 048 radial at 52 miles at 0204, estimating Grand Forks at 0238. Howard transmitted to the aircraft commander of Ivory 1 on the aircraft-to-aircraft frequency. "Tony, you reckon the Air Defense Command boys, those scope dopes, are hibernating?"

"Maybe so, Howard. With this kind of weather, I could understand it if they disappeared til spring. I sympathize with them. Looks completely white down there, and I don't believe that's white sand from the beach at Homestead."

"I think you're correct. Makes me shiver just thinking about the super cold temperatures they're having. Don't see how humans or animals live and function through such harsh conditions. And how do they start their vehicles and farm equipment? It's amazing to me. I was half grown before I saw a small snow in Louisville. Didn't care much for it even then. I sure wouldn't want to be transferred to a base in this part of the world."

"Yeah, know what you mean. I'm kinda like you—although my wife loves cold weather. Born and raised in upper Michigan peninsula . . .

"Howard, I suspect they'll hit us hard with everything they've got when we get closer to Grand Forks."

"I think you're right. We'll keep a sharp eye out for'em. We've got our guns ready just in case."

Howard switched to intercom and said, "Bob, I'll take the controls and let you relax and get something to eat if you'd like. After you've finished, suggest manning the gunnery radar."

"Roger that. Your aircraft now."

"I have the aircraft."

I've got the controls, but only temporarily. Gonna wake up my old buddy Auto and let him earn his pay. Leland will need him when he makes the bomb run at Radford.

Howard transmitted on the interphone, "Turning automatic-pilot on." He stretched his left arm across the walkway, pressed the automatic-pilot release button, pulled the unit downward, pressed the button again, and then pulled the unit outward until it locked in position. He located his Personal Automatic-pilot Checklist on his knee-pad and proceeded.

He looked at the instrument panel. *All three servo switches in disengage position, transfer control switch on pilot position.* He turned his attention to the automatic pilot controller. *Turn knob in detent, aileron trim knob centered, master switch off, automatic approach switch on automatic pilot.*

He checked the instrument panel to verify that the N-1 compass inoperative light was not illuminated, then changed his attention to the automatic pilot controller. *Master switch on.* He paused momentarily while the automatic pilot trim gyros updated. *Three trim indicators centered in reference position.* His eyes once again focused on the instrument panel. He selected the ENGAGE position on all three Servo Engaging switches with his left hand, then transmitted, "Automatic pilot is engaged."

Howard smiled and mused, *Just as I thought. Trimmed perfect for most efficient flight. Bob wouldn't have it any other way. Everything cleaned up, as it should be. Good man. . . . Good job. Fortunate to have him as my co-pilot. I'll miss him when he moves up to aircraft commander.*

At 0220, 120 miles south of Grand Forks, Howard switched to the bomb bay fuel tank and announced, "Operating on bomb bay tank."

Bob swallowed the last bite of his sandwich, emptied the milk carton, and stowed it in the waste bag. *Time to man the guns,* he thought. Just as his hand reached for the Seat Tilt and Rotation handle to turn his seat to face to the rear, the Gun Target Warning light on his instrument panel lit up—brilliant red. His heart skipped a beat. He thumbed the button on the control wheel and transmitted, "We've got company. I'm moving to the gun position."

CHAPTER TWELVE

Bob's chair locked in position facing the gunner's station. Although the fighters were friendly, the thought that other humans were searching for him always kicked in an additional squirt of adrenalin—not unlike when kids play hide-and-seek. His hands swarmed over three knobs on the Turret Control Panel, readjusting the altitude to 32,000 feet and the outside temperature to minus 44 degrees centigrade. He pressed his face tightly over the radar viewing hood to minimize glare from the cockpit lights. A red light located near the scope reaffirmed that the radar was detecting a target.

The radar scope's vertical sweep moved back and forth across the face of the scope, displaying a distinctive bright spot at eleven o'clock, 5,000 yards. While engaging the IFF button with his thumb, he stepped on his intercom transmitter switch and said, "Stranger at eleven o'clock, 5,000 yards, squawking mode three and closing rapidly."

"Roger. Thanks, Bob."

Howard relayed the information to Ivory 1. "Ivory 1, we're picking up a bogie on our tail less than 5,000 yards, closing rapidly—probably a Deuce."

"Rog, Ivory 2. We just picked him up also. Probably more in the pack."

"Concur. My co-pilot's all over it."

Bob smiled when he heard the compliment. While peering into the radar viewing hood, he placed his left hand on the Manual Antenna handle. After pressing the Action switch with his thumb, he moved the radar antenna beam to the target and released the Action switch. This locked on the radar for automatic tracking of the incoming aircraft. The A-5 Fire Control System Computer began calculating the target position, allowing for parallax, ballistic, and lead errors.

Bob stepped on the intercom switch and announced, "Radar lock-on, auto tracking . . . twelve o'clock, 1,500 yards, within effective firing range. Shall I turn on the buzzer?"

"Stand by, Bob," Howard replied. "Let's check with lead."

"Ivory 1, want us to turn the ECM on?"

"Ivory 2, stand-by."

After a slight pause, the aircraft commander of Ivory 1 transmitted, "Ivory 2, let them have some fun for now. As we approach the target at Radford, let's go full bore, jam and slam chaff. Confuse and abuse those scope-dopes."

"Rog, Ivory 1."

Bob peered into the viewing hood and pressed the search button. As the sweep updated the radar screen, another bright dot appeared at twelve o'clock and 4,000 yards. After target lock-on occurred and IFF was confirmed, he transmitted, "Another bogey at twelve o'clock, 4,000 yards, squawking mode three—fast overtake. Considering the speed, it's probably another Deuce." When he looked up, he saw the navigation lights of the first interceptor. The pilot maneuvered the F-102 Delta Dagger close enough to copy the tail numbers of Ivory 2, banked hard, and disappeared into the night. Shortly thereafter, the second supersonic F-102 passed very close to their wingtip and intercepted Ivory 1.

Both of those pilots probably called a splash on us, Bob thought. *If this was for real, Russian MiGs might not approach from the rear. . . . In that case, our only defense—our two .50-caliber cannons—would most likely be . . . useless.*

At 0429, Ivory 1 reported over Appleton, Ohio omni to the Indianapolis Center.

"Indianapolis, Ivory 1 over Appleton at 0429. IFR VFR on top climbing from 34,000 to 38,000 feet; estimate Pulaski 060 radial at twelve miles at 0450 Zulu, Charlotte next. Be advised, we're assuming a non-standard, five minute in-trail formation and increasing speed by ten knots." At this point, they were 200 nautical miles northwest of the target at Radford.

Ivory 1 transmitted to Howard, "We're increasing our speed ten knots. Turn your ECM on and drop some chaff. No doubt fighters are en route to attack us, so let's muck-up their radar."

"Ivory 2 copied. I'll reduce speed and make some small S turns if necessary to make our bomb away time of 0455."

Bob grinned. "Copied info on ECM and chaff," he transmitted, as he spun his chair clockwise to face the ECM and chaff dispensing controls. He switched both of the ECM transmitters from Standby to Transmit. Immediately, transmitters on each wingtip and thirteen transmitters located on the belly of the aircraft spewed out powerful energy in all directions and on the same frequency as the GCI radars. The Air Defense Command directors and radar operators located at strategic radar sites across the northeastern U.S. blinked, and a muffled sound echoed inside the dark radar rooms when their green scopes abruptly turned to a bright, whitish color, with occasional darker spokes emanating outward from the center of the display. Aircraft with an operational IFF could be partly discerned by a highly experienced director or operator, but aircraft operating with their IFF turned off or on standby, such as Ivory 2, would most likely go undetected.

When Bob activated the chaff dispenser, two small doors opened near the rear wheel wells. Small strands of aluminum foil streamed out of the B-47B into the frigid night and slowly floated earthward. The length and width of the foil was designed to ensure maximum radar reflectivity. The upper winds scattered the chaff, which would soon blossom into a large, bright area on the ADC radar displays similar to heavy weather in which an aircraft would not be discernable on their radar display without an IFF.

Meanwhile, seven miles below, the Air Defense Command senior directors were busy preparing their final battle plan in order to protect the target at Radford. Two interceptors had been scrambled and were now airborne. When the ECM started, the directors and radar operators turned off their primary radar to help reduce the clutter on their radar displays. In this configuration, the only aircraft displayed were those with an operational IFF.

Ivory 2 was approximately forty miles behind Ivory 1. This would provide enough time behind Ivory 1 to allow the Radford bomb plot operators to record both simulated bomb drops. Howard pushed the throttles forward as he leveled off at 38,000 feet. Within three minutes, the sleek jet's speed accelerated to mach point 83, indicating 260 knots with a true airspeed of 474 knots.

Ivory 2's IFF remained on standby and was not being displayed on the Air Defense Radar scopes. Neither was their primary target. The ECM made the primary radar, radar energy reflected from an aircraft and back to the radar antenna located on the ground, almost useless. In this configuration, Ivory 2 would most likely slip through the radar maze undetected and make a simulated bomb drop at Radford unmolested by the pesky fighter pilots. This would be the desired results if they were attacking a target in Russia. Of course, there was always the possibility that they would be spotted accidentally by a sharp-eyed intercept pilot.

Tucked in the nose of Ivory 2, Leland was busy preparing for the bomb run at Radford. Most of the mission planning, such as target, time, target study, route, target weather, and bomb data had been completed the previous day by Captain Winters. Leland stepped on the interphone button and transmitted, "Pre-IP checklist please."

Because Howard was flying the aircraft, Bob keyed his mike and replied, "Rog, stand-by." He pulled the checklist out of his equipment bag, then began.

"Compass."

"Unslaved."

"Oxygen control."

"One hundred percent."

"Local variation."

"Six degrees west."

"Lat and long counters."

"Reset."

"Altitude."

"Measured and computed 38,000."

"True airspeed."

"Hold 262 indicated air speed."

"Bombing mode switch."

"Sync."

"Pre-IP Checklist completed. Starting IP Procedure Checklist."

"Wind run on IP."

"Accomplished."

The checklist was abruptly interrupted by the high-pitched voice of the aircraft commander in Ivory 1.

"This is Ivory 1. We've got fighters all over us."

Howard grinned and keyed the mike. "Ha. Clear skies here. We've seen nothing. My guess is our ECM has befuddled their radar, and with my IFF off, they're unable to track us."

"Yeah, that makes sense. We just made the 25-mile call, and they're pulling away. The pack was heaviest from about 40 miles from the target til now."

"Rog, we'll keep a sharp lookout for 'em."

Bob continued with the checklist. "Position counters."

"Reset."

"IP turn."

"Completed."

"Magnetic variation."

"Checked."

"Bomb power switch."

"On."

"U-2 low pressure light."

"Out."

"Drop control switch."

"Delay."

"U-1 arming switch."

"Armed."

"U-2 rack lock handle."

"Unlocked."

"True heading."

"Checked."

"Bombing altitude."

"Set 38,000 feet."

"Pre-IP Checklist completed."

Howard scanned the instrument panel frequently for any hint of a problem. At Mach point 83, 38,000 feet, and with their current weight, the aircraft was very close to the high-speed buffeting envelope. Unexpected clear air turbulence could disturb the airflow over the wings and initiate buffeting. High speed buffeting can result in structural damage, particularly to the control surfaces.

From this point on until shortly after passing the target, Howard kept his right hand resting on the throttles. If buffeting did occur, he would immediately pull all six throttles backward to the idle position in order to quickly reduce speed. However, at this altitude and weight, reducing the speed too much could result in a low speed buffet or stall. Operating the aircraft safely in this critical zone required highly polished skills and in-depth knowledge of the aircraft and aeronautics.

Five minutes later, Leland transmitted, "Fifty miles out. Bomb run Checklist please."

"Offset switch."

"Checked out."

"Bombing altitude."

"Steady on altitude."

"Final lineup."

"Accomplished."

"Crosshairs."

"Position."

"Bomb run Checklist completed."

An Air Force bomb scoring unit, located in Radford, was busy preparing their equipment for the arrival of Ivory 2. Crammed into a converted railway passenger car parked on a side-track, they hustled to determine the accuracy and score of Ivory 1, reset the scoring equipment, and complete several sheets of documentation before the arrival of Ivory 2. Ivory 1 was over Radford at 0450 plus 30 seconds, thirty seconds late, which would decrease their score.

Two minutes and forty seconds after the Bomb run Checklist was completed, Leland requested the 25-mile Checklist.

Howard glanced at the Turn Controller on the automatic pilot to ensure the Turn Controller knob was correctly set in the Detent position, toggled the Turn Control switch to the K BOMB AUTOMATIC position, and transmitted, "PDI center, your aircraft." This action transferred directional control of the aircraft to the Radar Bombing and Navigation System.

Leland reached up to the Bomb Control Panel, flipped a switch to K2 Auto, and responded, "Roger, my aircraft, automatic."

Bob continued with the checklist. "O-23 power switch."

"On."

"Offset switch."

"Out."

Synchronization."

"Started."

"Final synchronization."

"Started."

"One hundred twenty seconds to go."

"Roger."

" . . . Twenty seconds to go. Tone ON and Bomb Drop and Release Switch Auto."

"Leland flipped the Bomb Scoring Tone switch to INITIATE and the Bomb Door and Release Control switch to K2 AUTO. "Roger, tone On and Release Switch Auto."

Ten seconds later, at 0455 Zulu, Leland transmitted, "Bomb away."

Howard looked at the left portion of his instrument panel as the red Bombs Away panel light glimmered. He shook his head and thought, *Apparently, we were never detected. This proves that our defense system has some serious flaws in it, but on the other hand, this system in our aircraft might give us the upper hand with the Russians. Hmm . . . Probably evens out in the long run.*

Howard transmitted on the interphone, "Turn Control to Pilot, now." He toggled the switch to PILOT and rotated the Turn Knob slightly clockwise for a shallow bank until the aircraft was stabilized on a 215-degree heading for the next checkpoint.

Leland didn't respond to Howard's transmission and none was expected.

Howard smiled. *Leland did a very nice job on the bomb run. Kept his cool. Should have a high score. Perfect timing. But right now, he's busier than a one-armed paper hanger with all that data collection and recording.*

"Bob, we're out of Indian territory, so turn the ECM transmitters off and stow the cannon. I'll read the checklist when you're ready."

"Roger that. Go ahead with the checklist."

"Rog, gun safety switch."

"Safe."

"Computer switch."

"Out."

"Manual holdback switch."

"Holdback."

"Intensity knob."

"Full counterclockwise."

"Low manual knob."

"Full counterclockwise."

"IF gain knob."

"Full clockwise."

"Range search limit knob."

"Full clockwise."

"Stow guns 180 degrees aft and elevation up."

"Completed."

"Selector switch."

"Off."

"Checklist complete."

"ECM transmitters off," Bob transmitted. "All chaff dispensed."

"Roger that. Getting rid of the chaff will make us lighter when we land."

"Yeah, and I bet it's giving those scope dopes a big headache. It will be several hours before it reaches the surface."

"You betcha. Bob, verify that we weren't intercepted approaching the target."

"That's correct, Major. No visual sightings. Nothing on the radar."

"Roger that. You ready for some stick time?"

"Yes, sir—always ready."

"Roger, standby for a second."

Howard flipped the automatic pilot switches for rudder, aileron, and elevator to Disengage, then reached across the walkway and toggled the auto pilot Master switch off and stowed the unit. While entering the time on his knee-pad, he transmitted, "Bob, it's your aircraft. Heading 215 for Charlotte. Let's reduce to 426 knots true airspeed."

"Rog, my aircraft. Reducing to 426 knots true airspeed."

"Leland, when you've caught up with your paperwork, resume navigational duties."

"Wilco, Major. Be a few more minutes."

"Rog."

"Atlanta Center, Ivory 1 estimating Charlotte at 0508, IFR, VFR on top descending out of 38,000 feet. Request block of 34,000 and 35,000 feet, in-trail non-standard formation."

"Ivory 1, roger. Maintain block of 33,000 through 35,000 feet. Report in the block and say approximate distance in-trail."

"Roger, Atlanta. Maintain 33,000 to 35,000. Wingman, Ivory 2 is approximately thirty miles in trail."

"Two copied."

Ivory 1 transmitted on the aircraft-to-aircraft frequency, "I'll descend to angels 34. Two, level at angels 35."

"Rog, angels 35 for Ivory 2."

"Leaving angels 38 for 35," Bob transmitted on the interphone, as he reduced power and pushed the elevator slightly forward.

Two minutes later, as Bob leveled off at angels 35, Howard transmitted to Ivory 1, "Ivory 2 level at angels 35."

"Roger, Ivory 2."

"Atlanta Center, Ivory 1 in block 33,000 to 35,000 feet."

"Ivory 1, Atlanta Center. Thank you. Report Charlotte."

"Ivory 1, wilco."

Howard stretched his arms, moved his feet out of the footrests, and flexed his legs to assist blood circulation. He scanned the fuel consumption on the Fuel Control Panel and thought, *Glad that's over. Should be a cake-walk from here to Homestead. Always concerned when those young jocks zip around me in their souped-up fighters.* He glanced at the instrument panel clock. *Be over Charlotte at about thirteen minutes after midnight. Charlotte . . . Nice town. Cornwalis's old stomping ground . . . I enjoyed reading* Rebels and Redcoats. *Turned out to be one of my favorite Christmas gifts from Vivian. She put the book in my luggage before I left for . . . Sidi Slimane, or was it Ben Gurie? Dang it, can't recall. Doesn't matter. Those Reflex missions are a real pain, especially on the family. Some battles of the Revolutionary War, like Camden, were gruesome. Absolute chaos. I'd rather be shot than hacked to death with a sword any day. A real disaster for the Patriots. Although it was a rather small battle, Kings Mountain, hmmm . . .* Howard gazed out of the cockpit toward his two o'clock position. *Not too far from here . . . struck me as being unique. The so-called rag-tag, Over Mountain Men, killed the British leader, Major Ferguson, destroyed or captured his small army and sent a strong message to the bewildered Patriots that the British weren't invincible. Fortunately for us, British brass squashed the use of an advanced rifle invented and tested by Ferguson . . . breech-loading, all-weather rifle that could be quickly loaded while in a prone position, very accurate and had exceptional range. It would take a lot of tough, dirty handling and still function. That rifle may have provided the British with the edge they needed to win. Wonder what the world would be like today if the Brits had won . . .* His stomach growled. *Time for a snack and smoke.*

Howard grabbed the seat adjustment handle with his right hand, moved his seat to a more comfortable position, and transmitted, "Bob, please hand me my thermos."

He set the thermos between his legs and reached for his pack of Lucky Strikes, pausing as he gazed at the twinkling lights of Charlotte in the distance at ten o'clock. *Believe we're a bit off course to the West. What am I doing?* He tossed the pack in his trash bag and smiled as he stared at his family photograph. *I'm quitting this goofy habit,* he thought. *I know you'll be happy.*

He poured the last of the coffee into a cup and handed the thermos to Bob. After swallowing a swig, he sat the cup in its holder, reached beneath his seat cushion, and pulled out the relief horn.

Leland transmitted on the interphone, "Through with the paperwork. I'll resume nav duties. Turn left to heading 190."

"Rog, coming left to 190 degrees."

CHAPTER THIRTEEN

hile Howard attended to his physiological needs, and Leland calculated their position, ground-based officers and airmen awaited their arrival. Approximately 200 miles to the southeast at Wilmington, North Carolina, men crammed into a radar room elbow to elbow, intently scanning their green Plan Position Indicator, or PPI radar scopes. The Air Defense Command's Ground Control Intercept, or GCI radar site at Wilmington, known as Wormwood, was one of many radar sites situated along the U. S. coast and, to a lesser extent, the interior of the U.S. Their mission was to detect an airborne invasion, presumably from Russia, scramble and vector fighter aircraft to intercept, and destroy the invaders.

Down the coast some 130 miles at North Charleston, South Carolina, the 792nd Aircraft Control and Warning Squadron, another GCI radar site known as Hemingway, was likewise on high alert. The regular mid-shift was on duty, assisted by several additional airmen and officers who were called in due to the SAC USCM exercise. All positions were operational. Some of the scopes were offset to scan a quadrant to the north and northwest of Charleston, where the B-47Bs were expected to penetrate Hemingway's assigned area of responsibility. A large Plexiglas plotting board occupied one end of the room. Azimuth lines etched 30 degrees apart extended outward from the center of the plotting board. Likewise, range circles placed twenty miles apart extended outward from the center of the plotting board. The center of the plotting board represented North Charleston, where the radar site was located. The coastline and other important items, such as major airports, the Savannah River Project boundary, large cities, and the Air Defense Identification Zone—or ADIZ—were also displayed. A video map depicted some of this information on the radar scopes.

The large, brightly lit plotting board was the centerpiece of the radar room. When viewed from the top dais at the opposite end of the room, it gave the Commanding Officer or Senior Weapons Director on duty an overall picture of the battle scene. Another smaller "tote board" attached to the plotting board listed all of the 444th FIS aircraft, their status, and the call sign of those on immediate alert status. Two airmen were assigned positions behind the board. When aircraft were detected by the radar operators, the information was relayed by interphone to the plotters. The position of the aircraft was forwarded using azimuth and distance from the radar site. The plotters had to be proficient in writing backwards in order to display the information so that it was presented correctly when viewed from the opposite side of the plotting board.

A typical amount of air traffic for an early Wednesday morning plodded along on the radar screens. Two air carriers, a DC-6 and a DC-7 en route from Miami to New York were east of Charleston over the Atlantic Ocean. During thunderstorm season, these aircraft would most likely be in radio contact with Hemingway for weather information. But tonight they found their own way in the excellent weather. A general aviation Cessna 310 heading home to Ashville, North Carolina was overhead the Orangeburg Omni. Two military transport aircraft based at Charleston, a C-54 and a C-121, appeared on the peripheral of the radar scopes east of Charleston. The navigators double checked their position, and the pilots had the Charleston Omni tuned in, hoping to be within the time and lateral limits to avoid an embarrassing intercept by an F-86L.

CAA Air Traffic Controllers at the Jacksonville Center forwarded flight plan data to Hemingway and other radar sites located in their jurisdiction. When the aircraft appeared on Hemingway's radar, they were declared friendly or unknown by Hemingway's Identification Officer, depending on the accuracy of their navigation. Drift too far off course to the right or left or show up too early or late and the Air Defense Command armed fighters would be scrambled to verify the aircraft's true identification.

Each aircraft were assigned a track number, and its position was updated approximately every ten miles. The radar scopes were positioned on three elevated rows or daises, each dais elevated higher than the one in front for improved visibility of the control room and plotting board. The highest dais, located in the back of the room opposite the plotting board, was reserved for senior officers and the Commanding Officer, if on duty.

The Commanding Officer, Major Edgar R. Armagost, had been on duty almost twenty hours—primarily because of the simulated wartime SAC USCM exercise. Another factor could have been his concern over a recent mid-air collision between two F-86L aircraft from the 444th Fighter Interceptor Squadron based at Charleston Air Force Base. Less than thirty-six hours earlier, one of his Intercept Controllers had been practicing intercepts with the two aircraft when they collided at 42,000 feet, fatally injuring one of the pilots. The controller was not responsible for the accident because the pilot making the intercept called "Judy" over the radio, meaning he either had visual or radar contact with the other aircraft and would complete the intercept. Even so, Major Armagost was deeply troubled and obviously felt an obligation to be on duty during this crucial nighttime exercise.

The thirty-seven-year old Commanding Officer was dressed in a Class A blue winter uniform adorned with several multi-colored medals and his command pilot wings. Armagost exuded the leadership, confidence, and necessary technical knowledge demanded by higher authority and respected by those subordinate to him. He loved his job, and it showed. He'd earned his rank the hard way. Reared on a rugged farm near the small coal-mining village of Reynoldsville, Pennsylvania, he had little desire to follow in his father's footsteps as a miner, or "underground farmer," as the locals referred to coal mining. He had greater things in mind. Greater aspirations. After graduating from high school, quite a feat in those days for a country boy, he journeyed to the Big Apple, where his hoped-for fortune failed to materialize. After working at several insignificant and low-paying jobs, he joined the Army.

After basic training, he was selected for flight school. Nine months later, on December 7, 1941, he graduated and was promoted to staff sergeant. Almost three years later, after accumulating many hours in various aircraft, he became the aircraft commander of a B-29 Super-fortress.

On August 15, 1945 during a night raid, he and his crew dropped 500-pound general purpose bombs on northern Japan's petroleum factories. On the way back to Guam, where he was based, he turned the controls over to a major who was along to keep current and earn flight pay. Armagost removed his parachute and slid into a tight, oval tube used to move about inside the aircraft. The steady droning of the four Wright Cyclone engines soon put him to sleep in this secluded part of the aircraft. He abruptly awoke to a thunderous clanging of metal and some of the aircrew jumping and shouting at the top of their lungs. Thinking they were under attack by a Zero, or having a serious mechanical problem, he scrambled out of the tube, grabbed his parachute, and asked the first person he saw, the radioman, what the commotion was about. That's when he heard the good news that Emperor Hirohito was throwing in the towel.

In order to keep the noise level at an acceptable level, the Hemingway Senior Weapons Director issued a verbal order for everyone to speak in a low tone. This resulted in a subdued hum as information was relayed from one position to the other, battle plans were reviewed, and assignments were made. Each day, a rotational schedule for the shift was prepared by a senior NCO for the lower ranking airmen. The position assignments for the radar operators and plotters were rotated each hour. Moving about the room and briefing the relieving airmen substantially increased the noise level during the position change, if not controlled. However, the rotation of positions was considered paramount. Fresh eyes were needed for scanning the radar scopes. Tired eyes or boredom can defeat even the most talented and diligent airman. Hopefully, even the smallest, nondescript bit of radar data would be detected by the young operators.

A strange humming sound emitted from the electronic equipment. Various colored lights and the green radar displays cast eerie shadows on tense faces, adding to the dramatic scene.

At 12:01 AM or 0501 Zulu, a young Airman Second Class at the Wormwood radar site toggled a three-way switch and scanned his PPI scope. He noticed an IFF target north of Charlotte. A recent graduate from basic training and a rapid course in radar operations at Keesler AFB, he found himself thrust into an important job of guarding the U.S.—a job with awesome responsibilities. To be sure the target was a real aircraft and not a phantom, he hesitated before calling the information to the plotter. Better to be sure than to get everyone excited over a false target. Experience, not the technical school, taught him that occasionally, a false or phantom IFF target would appear on the radar screen 180 degrees and at the same distance from the radar site as a real aircraft.

As the radar sweep moved clockwise and updated the face of his scope, the Mode 2 IFF painted on his scope again in a slightly different position, a mile or so farther south from the first paint. Wormwood's radar had picked up the Mode 2 of Ivory 1. The radar operator tried to swallow, but his dry mouth refused. He clicked on the interphone switch and transmitted to the plotter in a strained voice, "New target, 290 degrees . . . at 180 miles, southbound." The plotter used a yellow grease pencil, denoting an unidentified aircraft, started a track, and assigned track number PL1. A short time later, a low murmur emitted throughout the room when the Senior Weapons Director confirmed that PL1 was part of the USCM mission. This is what they had been anxiously waiting for. How many aircraft will show? Will their scopes become saturated with simulated Russian invaders? ECM and chaff? They knew twenty Stratojets were assigned to fly the Southern Belle mission. But only one officer in the radar room knew the answer, and he was forbidden to release the information. To do so would dilute the important training these airmen and officers would receive.

The Wormwood Senior Weapons Director huddled with the Intercept Controllers and quickly made a decision that their radar detected the aircraft too late for a successful intercept. Information would be cross-told to Hemingway, who was in a superior position to make a successful intercept. Wormwood's radar occasionally painted a weak and intermittent primary target approximately 33 miles behind track PL1. It was tracking southbound at the same ground speed as PL1.

However, Wormwood did not start a separate track on this aircraft, which was Ivory 2.

At 0505 Zulu, Hemingway received a cross-tell on target PL1 from Wormwood, plotted a track in yellow, and assigned it number PN17. At this time, Ivory 1 was ten miles north of Charlotte and beyond Hemingway's radar range. As the cross-tell was being made from Wormwood to Hemingway, the Senior Weapons Director at Wormwood called Hemingway. When the phone rang, Major Armagost answered. "Hemingway, Major Armagost."

"Captain Johnson, Senior Weapons Director at Wormwood. Major Armagost, our track PL1 is over Charlotte. We initially painted track PL1 too late for a realistic intercept from any of our bases. We have confirmed the IFF Mode 2 as being part of the Southern Belle USCM. There's two aircraft in-trail in the flight. We're cross-telling the information to you for your action."

While this conversation was in progress, Ivory 1 reported over Charlotte to Atlanta Center.

"Thanks, Captain Johnson." Armagost turned toward the plotting board and replied, "We've started a cross-tell track labeled PN17." He glanced at a radar scope. "We're not painting either aircraft on our radar at this time. Keep the cross-tell going until we advise that we have radar contact. We'll take it from here."

"Wilco. Thank you, sir." The line went dead.

Major Armagost briefed Captain Leach, the Senior Weapons Director, who was standing nearby. "Captain Leach, Wormwood has confirmed track PN17 is part of the USCM. Two aircraft, in-trail formation. They're not taking any action to intercept. Scramble at your discretion."

The young captain glanced at the plotting board, hesitated as he calculated in his mind the optimum time to get the fighters in the air, and headed in the best direction and speed for a successful intercept. Procrastinate and the fighters would be unable to catch the B-47Bs; scramble too early, and the fighters may be forced to return to base before an intercept due to low fuel. As a Senior Weapons Director and a pilot himself, Captain Leach made a quick decision based on solid judgment coupled with experience. After a quick analyzation, he nodded his head and said, "Yes, sir."

He picked up a red phone and buzzed Intercept Controller, Warrant Officer Ralph Wilson, seated in front of a radar scope two daises below. While in flight training, Wilson's T-28 had an engine failure. His knee was injured in the emergency landing, and he was medically disqualified to be a pilot. Soon afterward, he was assigned to a radar unit as a staff sergeant. After six months of experience, he was selected to become an Intercept Controller and was promoted to Warrant Officer after completing a stringent course in Air Defense Procedures.

Wilson punched the flashing button and answered, "Wilson."

"Ralph, track PN17 is part of the USCM. Two B-47s. Scramble three. Caution. Their groundspeed looks to be about 430 knots. Don't let 'em get too far south or you may not be able to cut'm off and make an intercept."

"Roger that."

Wilson released the phone button and placed his hand on the shoulder of his NCO assistant. "Sarge, scramble three for USCM, big spender, angels 20, buster, and button seven." In Air Defense Command jargon, these code words meant to scramble three fighters for USCM, initial heading north, climb to 20,000 feet at military power and contact Hemingway on radio channel seven.

"Yes, sir," the staff sergeant replied. "Got it." He moved the safety cover protecting the scramble button from an inadvertent alert. When he pushed the scramble button, a loud klaxon sounded in the alert hanger at the 444th FIS, in the Charleston control tower, and the air base weather department.

Two of the Pug Silver pilots were playing cards with two Pug Gold pilots. Several pilots were resting on bunks dressed in their flight suit and boots, ready to fly. Others were reading magazines, or updating their navigation charts, approach plates, and flight manuals.

The table slid sideways and the cards fell to the floor when the two Pug Silver pilots reacted to the klaxon. After about ten seconds, the sergeant in Hemingway issued the scramble instructions over a loud-speaker, which blared into the ears of the three Pug Silver pilots. They scampered down the steps, two at a time, toward their waiting Sabres. The crew chief's station was located on the hangar floor near the aircraft. When the pilots arrived at their aircraft, the crew chiefs had the APUs up and running.

Each pilot scaled the side of their F-86L and slithered into the cockpit, grabbing a helmet from its resting place on the windscreen as they settled into their seat. The crew chiefs were close behind the pilots and assisted with fastening the shoulder harness. The aircraft had already been preflighted, radio set to tower frequency, oxygen and radio lines plugged in, and IFF set on Mode 3. The pilots thumbed the auto start button as the crew chiefs hit the surface and pulled the wheel chocks. When the engines spooled up, the pilots turned their radios on and set the radar master switch to standby as the crew chiefs unplugged the APU.

The pilots fastened their leg straps, lap belt, slipped on their gloves, and lowered the canopy while taxiing. The control tower controller gave the flight priority over other aircraft and within five minutes after the scramble order, all three aircraft were at the end of the takeoff runway.

While the Pug Silver flight was lining up for takeoff, Hemingway's radar began to paint an IFF on Mode 2 from Ivory 1.

The location, altitude, and heading of Ivory 2 in reference to Hemingway's radar antenna was not ideal for reflecting radar energy. Although not designed for that purpose, the thin airfoil of the wings provided little radar reflectivity. Even so, if the aircraft was heading directly toward or away from the radar antenna, its slim silhouette would reflect even less energy. The reflective area would improve as Ivory 2 proceeded southbound and would reach its maximum when Ivory 2 was directly west of Hemingway's radar antenna.

At 0508 Zulu, after receiving several faint radar returns from Ivory 2, Captain Leach issued additional orders to another Intercept Controller. "Scramble three USCM, cowboy, angels 20, buster, button 6."

The klaxon sounded in the alert hanger less than five minutes from the last scramble. A bewildered look appeared on the faces of the three Pug Gold pilots because they hadn't expected another scramble order. At least not this soon. In less than three minutes, they were strapped in with turbines turning and tower clearance for immediate taxi and take-off. At 12:13 AM while Ivory 1 was checking in with Jacksonville Center, the three fighters screamed down the runway rattling windows and shaking walls in nearby homes. When they departed the Charleston airport traffic area five miles from the airport, Pug Gold 1 issued a frequency change. "Flight, let's go to Hemingway button 6."

"Two."

"Three."

CHAPTER FOURTEEN

"Hemingway control, Pug Gold."

"Roger, Gold Flight, read you five by. How me?"

"Roger, five by. Airborne, vectoring 270, climbing buster to 20. Squawking three normal."

"Roger. Let's continue your climb and go to button 8. If no contact, return this channel."

"Roger, Gold Flight; button 8."

"Gold 2."

"Gold 3."

"Hemingway, Pug Gold, button 8."

"Roger, Gold, read you five by. How me?"

"Roger, five by."

The Hemingway Intercept Controller queried Pug Gold 1 if the IFF was transmitting on Mode 3 normal power.

"Roger, Gold Flight. Understand squawking 3 normal. Affirmative?"

The pilot of Pug Gold 1 glanced at his IFF control panel and responded, "That's affirmative."

The pilot of Pug Gold 2 reached over to his right to the IFF control panel, turned the IFF selector knob back and forth, and reset it on mode 3. A small tear in his thin leather glove snagged on the knob.

"Two, you tied on to 1?"

The pilot stared out of the canopy, then down at his radar. Thumbing the microphone button on the control stick, he transmitted, "Tally-ho."

"Three, you tied on to 2?"

"Tally-ho."

The controller instructed Pug Gold Flight to climb to angels 30, or 30,000 feet, and increase power to afterburner, leaving angels 15.

"Roger, let's go up to 30,000 feet. Let's climb buster to about 15, gate the rest of the way."

"Roger, going buster to 15 and gate to 20 . . . gate to 30."

The intercept controller placed a clear plastic intercept aid on the face of his off-set radar display. The aid was inscribed with various angles and other data, which assisted in predicting the intercept point. Based on that calculation, he revised the instructions to gate or afterburner at the current altitude rather than angels 15.

"Gold Flight, let's go gate up to 30 thousand."

"Roger. You want us to go now?"

"Roger."

"Roger, going gate now. Acknowledge."

"Roger, 2 holding 1."

"Roger, 3."

Pug Gold 2 queried Pug Gold 3. "How's it coming, Three?"

After a nineteen-second pause, Gold 3 responded, "Roger."

"Two going gate."

The Hemingway Intercept Controller quizzed Pug Gold 2. "Two, you tied on to One now?"

"Two affirm."

"Roger. Three on Two?"

"Three has tally-ho."

"Roger. What altitude, One?"

"One passing angels 11."

"Roger."

"What's our range to target now?"

"Roger. The target is being cross-told to us from Wormwood present time. He's about a 105 miles out from Charleston."

"Roger."

"Gold Flight, let's turn in-trail starboard to 360."

"Roger, Gold Flight; in-trail starboard to 360."

"Roger, Two."

"Three."

"Gold Flight, at present time he seems to be tracking about 180 to 190 heading."

"Gold, roger."

Major Howard Richardson and his flight crew were completely oblivious to any of this fast-paced action carried out on their behalf. He yawned and stretched his arms. *My butt is getting tired. Been a long ride. I hope we never take a flight similar to this one for real. We'd probably meet the Russians en route to bomb our cities. Utter madness. What's the name the press gave it . . . uh, assured destruction or something similar . . . mutual, mutual assured destruction. That's it. MAD. The press probably got it right. If only we could put the genie back in the bottle. The bomb was definitely needed to end the war with Japan and save . . . probably millions of lives on both sides. But now, we just keep escalating, tit for tat . . .* He gazed down toward the bomb bay where the Mark 15 thermonuclear bomb lay silently in its straps. *Probably got enough of those babies to destroy everything and everybody several times over. But I doubt if we can stop now . . . maybe never . . . .*

Should be back on the ground at Homestead by two, complete the paperwork, debrief, and be home by four. Take a short cat-nap and then have some quality time with the family. Maybe play some cow pasture pool tomorrow . . . invite Bob and Leland if I play. Gotta make a note in the log about the relief horn being used . . . The ground crew really loves that entry. Ha!

He scanned the instrument panel, then focused his eyes on the rear view mirror. *Bob is intently watching over this bird. Got eyes like an eagle. Great feel for the aircraft.* He yawned and stretched his arms again. *Man, I could sure use some coffee . . . Haven't heard from Leland in a while.* He thumbed the interphone button on the control wheel and said, "How we doing down there, Leland?"

"Missed our checkpoint. Too far west of Charlotte. Trying to get us back on course. Definitely want to stay out of the Savannah River Project Prohibited Area."

"Concur, Leland. Those ADC boys might send up some fighters with intent to do harm."

"Know what you mean. Bob, turn farther left to 170 degrees."

"Roger, coming left to 170."

The Intercept Controller at Hemingway informed Pug Gold 1 that Hemingway's height-finder radar indicated Ivory 2 was at angels 31.4. For unknown reasons, he assumed that Ivory 2 was higher, at angels 34.

"We have him at 31.4 angels. He's probably up about 34. Suggest you go up to about 35 angels present time."

"Roger, Gold will climb to 35 angels."

"What angels now, One?"

"Gold 1, angels 17."

"Roger."

The Hemingway Intercept Controller advised the Gold Flight that their IFF was weak.

"Gold Flight, check your parrot, please. I'm getting rather weak skin paint . . . uh . . . parrot paints on you."

"Roger, Gold 1 steady 360."

'Roger, Gold."

"Gold 1 passing angels 20. Gold Flight, check oxygen and fuel."

"Roger, Two."

"Roger, Three."

The pilots routinely sucked two or three times through their mask while watching the oxygen flow gauge change from black to white, indicating normal pressure and flow, then glanced at their fuel gauges to verify that fuel was being used from the drop tanks.

"Two steady."

"Roger, Two."

"Three steady."

"Roger, Three. What angels now, One?"

"Gold 1 passing angels 23."

"Roger. One, you continue your turn to 270."

"Roger, 270 for One. That in-trail?"

"That's for One only. Roger, let's make that 270 for all of Gold Flight, and Two and Three, you can displace yourselves off to the left."

"Roger, understand you want that to be an in-place turn."

"Roger, let's make it in-place now to 27."

"Two turning now, Three."

Gold 3 responded, "Roger."

"Gold 1 steady 270."

"Two steady."

The Intercept Controller advised Pug Gold 1 of the position of Ivory 2, which was 35 degrees right when viewed from the pilot's seat. This provided the pilot a general direction in which to search on their radar screen for the target or manually move the radar antenna so that it pointed in the general direction of Ivory 2.

"Roger 1, you should have him about 35 degrees starboard now at 35 miles."

"Gold 1, roger."

"What angels now, One?"

"Gold 1, angels 30."

Leaving angels 30, Pug Gold 1 reduced power out of afterburner but failed to communicate with the other two pilots. Pug Gold 2 noticed he was overtaking Pug Gold 1 and reduced power.

"Two backing off."

Gold 3 responded, "Rog."

"One, continue your turn to about 260."

"One roger, 260."

The Hemingway Intercept Controller advised Pug Gold 3, "Number Three, I have you on the line."

"Rog."

"Gold 1, steady 260. How many fighters . . . uh . . . how many bogies is it?"

"Roger, I've only got . . . two bogies in the track. Should be . . . "

"Roger, they flying close formation?"

"Roger, I'm only painting one, and he's coming in weak right now. Gold Flight, let's all turn port to 260."

"Roger, Two."

"And Three."

"Gold Flight, make that all port to 250."

"Roger, Gold Flight in place 250."

"Roger, Two."

"Three."

"One steady 250."

"Roger, when steady 250, One, you'll have him about 40 degrees starboard at 25 miles."

Pug Gold 1 most likely painted Pug Silver 3 or possibly received electronic interference on his radar and transmitted, "One, roger, no joy . . . One has a paint, a paint about 25 degrees port at 25."

The Hemingway Intercept Controller initially agreed with Pug Gold 1 that the target was port or to the left of Pug Gold 1 but quickly realized the mistake and corrected it.

"Roger it's him . . . say again, port?"

"Affirmative."

"Roger, you should be heading 250. Affirmative?"

"Roger, I'm steady 250."

"Roger, you should have him about 40 degrees, make it 50 degrees to your starboard about 21 miles."

"Roger, no joy."

Pug Gold 1 pilot moved his left hand to the Radar Antenna Hand Control while holding the control stick with his right hand. He pressed the Action Switch and moved the control to the right until the antenna moved 50 degrees right. He released the Action Switch. The radar antenna moved clockwise so that it pointed in the general area of the target, which was Ivory 2.

"Angels, 1?"

"Roger, 1 level angels, level 35."

"Say again, please."

"One is level angels 35."

"Roger, you should have him about 50 degrees starboard now at 19."

"That's affirmative. I have a contact about 40 degrees starboard at 16."

"That's him . . . Two, you should have him 40 degrees starboard at about 18."

Pug Gold 2 glanced down at his radarscope, thumbed his mike, and replied, "Roger, no joy." Leveling at 35,000, the Pug Gold 2 pilot adjusted the power and trimmed the Sabre for level flight. He compared the artificial horizon on the radarscope with the main artificial horizon on the instrument panel. The two didn't match. He reached down with his left hand to the Radarscope Control Panel and adjusted the artificial horizon to level flight. The IF Gain knob on the Radar Control Panel was tweaked so that the sensitivity of the radar receiver presented a clearer presentation. He was ready for action.

The Hemingway Intercept Controller continued. "Three, about 25 miles for you, 35 degrees starboard."

"Roger, Three, no joy."

"Two, you're about seventeen miles out. Look about 30 degrees starboard."

Pug Gold 1 pilot moved a switch on the Radar Control Panel from Long Pulse to Short Pulse. This decreased the interval between the listening period, increased the number of radar transmissions for a given time period, and presented a superior target on the radar display.

Pug Gold 1 pilot advised Hemingway that he had a Judy, meaning his radar had "locked-on" the target and that he would complete the intercept.

"One has a Judy."

"Roger, Judy for One."

Pug Gold 1 unintentionally transmitted that his steering dot was below the center of the reference circle on his radar display.

"I have a fly down indication."

"Say again."

"Disregard."

"Two, you have a contact yet?"

"Negative."

"Understand, Judy for Two?"

"Negative Two. No contact, no joy."

"Roger. You heading 250, Two and Three?"

"I am, Two."

"Three affirm."

"Roger. You should have him about 50 degrees starboard at about fifteen miles . . . Two, any luck?"

The pilot of Pug Gold 2 lowered his head and peered at his six-inch, round radar scope located in the lower center of his instrument panel. A bright spot was displayed on the screen near the position given by Hemingway. He thumbed his mike and replied, "Two, roger contact."

"Roger contact. Three, you got him about 50 degrees starboard at 16."

"Three turning in."

The pilot of Pug Gold 2 turned right 15 degrees toward Ivory 2. He grabbed the Antenna

Hand Control with his left hand while holding the stick steady with his right hand. His leather glove snagged on the Antenna Hand Control as he moved his finger toward the Action Switch. He frowned, quickly removed both gloves, and tossed them in the map case.

He squeezed the Action Switch on the Antenna Hand Control with his index finger, moving the control to align the vertical radar sweep with the blip of Ivory 2. Then he moved the Antenna Hand Control back and forward. This moved his radar antenna beam up and down to "spotlight" the target. When the center of the radar beam strikes the aircraft, the blip becomes brighter, signifying the best angle in which to aim the antenna. Next, he thumbed the Range In-out Switch until the Range-Gate Marker coincided with the radar blip. The radar sensed the selected target and automatically locked on the blip. He released the Action Switch, and the radar went into automatic track operation. The Pug Gold pilot will complete the intercept without further assistance from the Intercept Controller.

The radar scope automatically changed to an attack presentation consisting of a steering dot, time-to-go outer circle, a small inner reference circle, a closing rate scale, artificial horizon, and other less critical indicators.

Pug Gold 2 had a Judy but did not inform Hemingway due to frequency congestion. He made small turns and changes in altitude to keep the steering dot in the middle of the one-inch diameter reference circle. A magnetic tape recorder, located in the aft end of the canopy, automatically began to record the data displayed on the radarscope. Known as NADAR, it recorded the attack phase from lock-on to pull-out. This information can be used later at briefings to discuss pilot technique and as a training aid.

"One, you still have your Judy?"

"One, roger."

"Three, you should be about 50 degrees starboard now at 17."

"Three, roger, has a contact."

"Roger, Three has a contact."

The steering dot on Pug Gold 2's radar moved out of the circle to the left. Pug Gold 2 transmitted as he made a shallow left turn, "Two converting port."

"Say again."

"Two converting port."

"Roger."

"Three lost contact."

"Roger, Three. You should be about thirteen miles out, about 40 degrees starboard, now."

"Roger, Three has a Judy."

"Roger, Three has a Judy . . . Two, do you have a Judy?"

"Two affirm."

Leland calculated Ivory 2 was clear of the Savannah River Project Prohibited Area and transmitted, "Bob, turn right to heading 225."

"Roger coming right to 225."

Pug Gold 1 observed Ivory 2 turn right to the southwest and advised Hemingway.

"I believe your bogey's turned, Hemingway."

"Roger. May be, Gold Flight."

After Ivory 2 completed the right turn to a heading of 225, the tail of the aircraft was pointed toward Hemingway's radar. In this configuration, the Stratojet's fuselage presented a profile with a diminished area to reflect Hemingway's radar energy.

"We're not getting a very good paint on him. He looks like he's turning probably to the southwest a little, to the starboard."

"Roger, Three."

The steering dot in Pug Gold 2's radar moved to the right when Ivory 2 turned to a heading of 225. Pug Gold 2 turned right until the dot was re-centered.

CHAPTER FIFTEEN

Pug Silver 1 made an identification pass on Ivory 1. The co-pilot noticed the F-86L that had snuggled up close enough to read the tail numbers of Ivory 1. The co-pilot of Ivory 1 immediately advised Ivory 2.

"Ivory 1 under fighter attack by a single F-86. He came in from left to right."

Howard was casually reviewing the Savannah River Project Prohibited Area on a navigational chart when Ivory 1 called. He dropped the chart in his lap and straightened up in his seat. Startled, he thumbed the control wheel switch and transmitted, "Ivory 1, verify fighter attack."

After a short pause, the co-pilot transmitted, "That's affirmative, and another F-86 just made a pass on us."

"Roger that. We'll keep our eyes peeled. What the heck's going on? This is not supposed to happen."

The aircraft commander of Ivory 1 transmitted, "That's affirmative, Howard. Guess we'll find out when we get back to Homestead. We may have been briefed incorrectly, or perhaps there was some sort of mix-up at headquarters. Could be intentional to see how we react to an unexpected intercept at night."

"Yeah. Could be, but I'll go with the mix-up."

Pug Gold 3 maneuvered to a point less than a mile to the left of Pug Gold 2 and wisely inquired whether Pug Gold 2 had visual contact.

"Two, do you have tally-ho Three, nine o'clock position?"

The pilot of Pug Gold 2 had been keeping a close eye on Pug Gold 3 with his peripheral vision and replied, "Roger, gotcha boy."

"One's in a tail chase."

"Roger 1."

"Same-o for Two."

"Same-o for Three."

"Gold 1 will make an ID."

"Roger."

The time-to-go reference circle on Pugh Gold 1's radar began to shrink. He informed Hemingway that simulated rocket launch would occur in ten seconds.

"One has ten seconds to go."

"Roger, One."

"He is about angels 35 point 5."

"Roger, understand 35 point 5."

Pug Gold 1 informed Hemingway of a simulated kill.

"One splash."

Bob saw movement out of his right eye and turned his head in time to observe Pug Gold 1 pass close underneath and pull up in a right turn. He transmitted over the interphone in an uneasy tone, "F-86 at three o'clock, our altitude."

Howard glanced to his right and observed the navigational lights of Pug Gold 1. Howard transmitted over the aircraft-to-aircraft frequency, "Ivory 2 under attack, single aircraft."

The Hemingway Intercept Controller issued instructions to Pug Gold 1.

"Roger, let's break starboard 090."

"Roger, starboard 090."

Pug Gold 2 inquired, "Which way you breaking?"

"Roger, starboard 090."

"Roger."

"Three's turning in."

The pilot of Pug Gold 2 was probably having trouble with his radar. He volunteered to break off the intercept if Pug Gold 3 had a good radar lock on Ivory 2.

"Roger boy . . . if you look like you got a real good one, Jim, I'll break off."

"Negative, it's a tail chase."

"Rog."

Unidentified person at Hemingway gave a radio test count. "Hemingway testing, one, two, three, four, five, five, four . . . "

The pilot of Pug Gold 2 transmitted, and Pug Gold 3 responded.

"This guy's really going."

"I know it."

The Hemingway Intercept Controller requested the status of Pug Gold 2.

"Gold 2, you still chasing?"

"Two. I'm still after him."

"Rog."

The circle on Pug Gold 2's radar display collapsed to a smaller circle, indicating twenty seconds until simulated rocket firing. He double-checked to make sure the 24 Mighty Mouse rockets were tucked in the belly of the Sabre, the safety switch was ON, and transmitted, "Two's about twenty seconds."

"Roger, Two."

The pilot of Pug Gold 2 glanced up from the radar display when the Sabre suddenly began to shake and the wings rolled violently back and forth. He was surprised because the air had been extremely smooth the entire flight. Several freshly made contrails were clearly visible in the bright moonlight. He glanced down again and intently watched the time to go circle shrink to ten seconds. At 4.5 seconds, he squeezed the trigger. The circle was replaced with a small horizontal bar. He kept the wings level using the artificial horizon displayed on the radarscope. A large X emerged on the radarscope, indicating simulated rocket launch. He raised his head, banked the Sabre to the right, and began a standard breakaway pattern.

About ten seconds into the turn, the rear end of a B-47 loomed a few short yards away. It should have been a mile or so ahead. Instead, it was practically in his windscreen. The information was transmitted to his brain in a millisecond. His brain initially refused to accept the impossible. Refusal. He flinched but instinctively pushed the control stick full forward and full to the right in a valiant attempt to miss the B-47B. The agile F-86L reacted almost instantly, banking farther right in a nose-down configuration that miraculously missed the tail of the B-47B. But it was too late. The leading edge of the F-86L's left wing struck the rear of the B47's right wing near the auxiliary fuel tank, cutting a gash in the B-47B's wing three feet wide and three feet deep. The aft main spar was severed. The upper and lower stress plates for the auxiliary fuel tank and the right aileron and flaperon were extensively damaged.

The grinding and screeching sound of metal slicing into other metal penetrated Pug Gold 2's helmet. The sudden deceleration flung his head and arms forward as if he were a rag doll. Loose material and dust obscured the cockpit.

The damaged fuel tank separated from the B-47B. Eight feet of the Sabre's left wing and the drop tank separated, slamming into the B-47B's aft fuselage, severing the empty aft main fuel tank, destroying forms and bulkheads, and strewing smaller parts into the rear fuselage. The debris bounced off the fuselage and struck the vertical stabilizer and the starboard horizontal stabilizer. A piece of the F-86L's wing imbedded in the B-47B's vertical stabilizer. Fuel from the F-86L's ruptured wing tank exploded in a horrific fireball.

The cockpit of Ivory 2 glowed as bright as day as the deafening, grinding sound of the collision filled the cockpit simultaneously with a near bone-breaking jolt. Newton's three laws of motion kicked in—more so with "For every action there is an equal and opposite reaction." The impact knocked the B-47B into a skid 30 degrees counterclockwise and forced the starboard side of the aircraft down into a 12-degree starboard bank. The gyros in the cockpit spun frantically, trying to compensate for the sudden change in direction and attitude. Normally, with the right wing down and the left wing up, the aircraft would turn right, not left.

The navigational chart flew out of Howard's lap into the right side of the cockpit, partially covering the canopy. His head snapped toward his right shoulder, and his arms and legs bent in a precarious manner sending a sharp pain to his neck and left shoulder. The family photograph, cigarette butts, ashes, and other small bits of material and dust hidden in crevices for years were flung about the cockpit.

Bob's hands were torn from the control wheel. As his body reacted to the impact, he immediately grabbed the control wheel and tried to make sense of the instruments. Down below, Leland was affected more severely than the other crew members because his seat was farther forward from the impact zone. When the collision occurred, he was measuring the distance to the next turning point with calipers. The calipers jumped out of his hand like a scared bull frog. His navigational chart and pencil lodged on the starboard side of the fuselage, flung by an unseen force. His arms, legs, and head were violently jerked to his right.

The pilot of Pug Gold 2 struggled against the high G forces to locate the ejection handles. He inadvertently keyed the mike, resulting in a clicking sound recorded on Hemingway's recorder. A fraction of a second later, the Sabre's fuselage struck the rear of the B-47B's number six engine. The engine's rear mount broke loose from the underside of the wing, leaving the engine connected only by the front mount. The engine dangled from the wing in a 45-degree nose-up attitude. The fuel line remained intact, and the engine continued to produce thrust, but in an undesirable, downward manner. Two thirds of the F-86L's starboard wing broke away followed by the wing center section with the main landing gear still attached. The B-47B's horizontal stabilizer slammed into the Sabre's debris field but somehow remained intact—a testimony to its rugged structure. Gold 3 was temporarily blinded by the bright flash at one o'clock. He suspected something was terribly wrong and transmitted, "Two, do you read?"

Negative response.

Thirty-five miles south of the collision, the co-pilot of Ivory 1 observed a bright flash in his peripheral vision at five o'clock. Ivory 1 made a right turn for a better view, decided they could be of no assistance, and continued on course. When Pug Gold 1 was halfway through his starboard turn to heading 090, he also witnessed the explosion at three o'clock but did not immediately respond.

The remainder of the F-86L was clear of the B-47B but was engulfed in an inferno. The noxious odor of smoke and jet fuel seeped under the pilot's facemask. Somehow, he managed to locate the starboard ejection handle. There was no time to prepare for ejection. Ideally, he would have been sitting erect in the seat of an aircraft in level flight, chin tucked in, helmet pressed against the headrest, heels well back against the seat, and arms braced in armrests. But he was in a tumbling, burning fuselage without wings.

He pulled the handle, which ejected the canopy and exposed the ejection trigger. Pausing momentarily, going through the procedure as he had practiced many times in his mind, he squeezed the trigger. Miraculously, the ejection seat system was undamaged. The exploding 75-millimeter canon shell careened his seat out of the cockpit into the frigid, thin air. Seconds earlier, he was in a comfortable air-conditioned and pressurized cocoon. He tumbled earthward, still strapped in his seat, his limbs flailing as he slowly regained his wits. Air was rushing by very fast and his extremities, especially his exposed hands, were quickly losing their dexterity and feel. But the lieutenant was a survivor. Everything under his power would be utilized to overcome this incident.

Slowly, he recalled the emergency ejection procedures etched somewhere deep within his brain. At 33,000 feet, oxygen is scarce, and his brain would begin to deteriorate in a short time. His fingers were almost useless. After two or three attempts, he successfully pulled the small knob or "green apple" on the oxygen bottle attached to his parachute. The seal broke. Oxygen under high pressure rushed into his mask. He gulped, coughed, inhaled, and filled his burning lungs with pure oxygen.

The Hemingway Intercept Controller became concerned that his radar presentation was degraded because the aircraft were almost out of his radar range and suggested that the pilots keep a sharp lookout for other aircraft.

"Gold Flight, be advised, I'm not getting very good paints on you or the target right now, so if it's any . . . uh . . . if you suspect any . . . uh . . . suggest you keep heads up."

Pug Gold 3 virtually screamed into the mike, and in the confusion, called Hemingway, Basketwool, a GCI radar site at nearby Aiken, South Carolina.

"Basketwool, there was an explosion or something. This is . . . Gold 2 . . . was a bright flash. I can't read Gold 2."

The Hemingway Intercept Controller understandably believed that it was Gold 2 making the transmission and replied, "Say again, Gold 2."

"Gold 3. Gold 3 here. It's a mid-air collision."

"You say you have a mid-air collision?"

"Roger, Mayday, Mayday."

"Roger, understand."

The Hemingway Intercept Controller jumped up and shouted, "I've had a mid-air," and sat back down in front of his radar display. Captain Leach quickly gathered the preliminary information about the collision, and Armagost informed Divisional Headquarters.

Pug Gold 1 apparently overheard all the transmissions and was also confused as to what had actually transpired.

"Hey, Gold 3, was that Gold 2?"

"Roger, Gold 2. I saw a bright explosion, and it's going on down now, apparently on fire."

"Roger, I had . . . uh . . . I saw an explosion also. Did he hit the B-47?"

"Apparently. I can't . . . The B-47 is gone. I have no contact on him."

"Well, Roger. Well, don't fly where you'll hit his parachute."

"Roger, I'm out the way."

Howard sat upright, shook his head, and grabbed the vibrating control wheel. He thumbed the interphone and transmitted, "I have the aircraft. Bob and Leland, say your status."

"Roger, Major," Bob responded. "You have the aircraft. I'm groggy but seem to be basically okay. What happened?"

"Stand by, Bob. Leland, you okay?"

"Yes, sir. Shaken, but I seem to be all here. Can't say the same for some of my equipment."

Howard's eyes danced over the instrument panel, trying to make sense of conflicting data. He remembered a basic rule to use in emergencies and muttered to himself, *Ignore all outside interferences. Fly the aircraft, Howard. Fly the aircraft.* He leveled the wings using outside visual references. Airspeed was rapidly decreasing. He pushed the nose

over, added power, and transmitted, "Apparently one of the interceptors hit us. Bob, what can you see back there?"

"Number six is almost torn off the wing; the starboard drop tank is
missing, and I can see something, probably metal, sticking up on the
starboard wing. Port side appears normal."

When Bob mentioned the number six engine, Howard immediately
scanned the instruments, jerked his head around, and looked at the
damaged engine. He tried to pull the throttle fully backward to the
cutoff position. The throttle cable was misaligned or damaged. Howard
pulled with his full strength to move the throttle to the stopcock or cutoff position, which should cut off the fuel. It wouldn't budge. He gritted
his teeth and yanked on the throttle. Nothing. His years of experience
and over 1,000 hours of flight time and training in the B-47B kicked in.
He thought for a second, reached up to the top of his instrument panel,
and pulled the Fire Shutoff switch for number six engine. This action
prevented fuel and oil flow to number six engine.

Howard advised the other crew members, "Unable to stopcock. I've
pulled the fire-button. Number six is shutting down. Review the bailout
procedures in your mind just in case. Masks on, 100% oxygen." While
placing his oxygen mask on his face, he transmitted, "For now, let's see
if this thing will continue to fly. I don't know what your thoughts are,
but I'm not anxious to jump into a freezing swamp—especially at night."

"Hemingway, Gold 1."

"Roger, Gold 1, go Mayday please."

The Gold 1 pilot reached over to the IFF panel with his right hand,
selected emergency on the IFF, acknowledged the Mayday instructions,
and asked distance and direction to Charleston AFB.

"Roger, what's our pigeons now?"

"Roger, I have you about 75 miles out."

"Roger, Gold 1 is on Mayday."

Gold 3 pilot was obviously shaken by what he had just witnessed
and again referred to Hemingway as Basketwool.

"Basketwool, Gold 3 here. I'm in a starboard orbit over the scene,
over."

"Gold 1, you're sixty miles out now."

"Hemingway, Gold 1."

"Roger 1, go ahead."

"I'll squawk Mayday, and we don't want to fly right around the area where he bail—where he might have bailed out. We might fly into his parachute."

"Roger . . . One and Three all squawking Mayday?"

"One is squawking Mayday, roger."

"Three is Mayday, affirmative."

CHAPTER SIXTEEN

oward and his flight crew didn't overhear any of the Pug Gold or Hemingway radio transmissions because they were not monitoring that radio frequency.

Howard quickly scanned his instruments. The indicated airspeed had dropped to 220 and stabilized. Not dangerously low at their altitude under normal circumstances, but this was anything but normal. Number six engine was producing a considerable amount of drag and negative thrust. The starboard wing tank was missing, and the starboard wing had suffered severe damage that was causing some of the vibration and drag. Howard suspected there was additional damage because of the unusual way the aircraft performed.

He kept the aircraft in a nose-down attitude, trading altitude for speed. In order to keep the aircraft from turning right toward the damaged wing and engine, he used a considerable amount of left rudder. Howard decided to remove the port wing tank in order to reduce weight and drag.

He turned the IFF on and switched the mode selector to Emergency. After analyzing his options for a short time, he transmitted, "Bob, get on guard and declare an emergency. Leland, give me a heading to the closest base, probably Hunter, and let me know when we're clear of populated areas so I can jettison the port fuel tank."

Bob selected 243.0 on his radio panel, thumbed his mike, and transmitted, "Mayday, Mayday, Mayday, this is Ivory 2, mid-air collision."

The startled control tower controllers at Hunter Air Force Base glanced at the speaker, then at the senior controller. The transmission was clear, but their brains didn't initially accept the information. Gradually it soaked in. This was real. Not a drill. The senior controller, a technical sergeant with combat experience, stepped forward, toggled the guard frequency switch to ON, picked up the mike, and transmitted, "Aircraft calling Mayday. Hunter tower, say again call sign, type, location."

"Roger, this is Ivory 2, B-47B, approximately fifty miles northwest. We were hit by another aircraft. Have severe damage, number six engine shut down."

"Roger, understand Ivory 2. The weather is clear, visibility fifteen miles, winds calm, altimeter 30.17. Construction on runway overruns with 18-inch drop-off on runway 9 and 27."

Leland transmitted, "Heading 120 for Hunter. Radar shows clear of populated areas for next thirty miles."

"Roger, thanks Leland."

Howard cautiously started a very slow left turn toward a 120 heading. The aircraft pulled to the right, making a left turn more difficult.

More rudder for a semi-coordinated turn, almost full aileron.

Keep the ball centered as much as possible . . . aileron must be damaged. Snags on something, hesitates when I exert pressure. Lord only knows what problems we have.

Bob grabbed the Emergency Checklist from his bag and located the Wing Tank Jettison section. "Major Richardson, for empty wing tank, flaps up, indicated air speed 155 to 300."

While Bob was advising Howard of the jettison procedures, the radio blared, "Ivory 2, Hunter Tower. Did you copy, over?"

Howard ignored the call from the Control Tower and checked the airspeed indicator, which had increased to 230 in the descent. He removed his right hand from the control wheel, pushed the switch guard up for the left hand tank, and moved the switch to the Release position. This action activated a solenoid, which ejected the wing tank tail-cone. The tail-cone deployed a ribbon-type drag chute, which pulled the tank backwards. The tank and strut fell free; cover plates rotated and closed the fuel lines. The flight crew felt the aircraft yaw slightly to the right when the tank jettisoned. Because of the missing port tank, more pressure was needed on the left rudder to maintain a steady heading. Normally, trim would be used to relieve the pilot from maintaining the balance with his foot, but Howard was reluctant to use trim. If the aircraft suddenly entered into an unusual attitude, he could relieve the rudder pressure immediately by simply removing his foot.

The oxygen revived the Pug Gold 2 pilot enough to make rational decisions despite the continuous pitching and tumbling of the non-aerodynamic seat. The flaming wreckage of his aircraft streaked earthward not far below. Burning debris, scattered surface lights, and occasionally the moon flashed through his line of sight as he tumbled end over end. The constant movement of the seat made it difficult to judge his height from the sparse light on the ground. He was not sure how long it had been since he'd ejected. He definitely did not want to crash into the ground with a perfectly good parachute strapped to his back. He made a decision to stop the free-fall despite the training manuals that recommended remaining in the seat until at least 12,000 feet, allowing an altitude sensor to automatically eject the seat and open the parachute. But the training manuals didn't mention a gyrating ejection seat or how to react in a situation where you are uncertain of your altitude. Could he trust his life to an automatic system? Would it function?

With great effort, using his numb, almost stiff fingers, he unlatched the lap belt and shoulder harness. He shoved the seat backwards with both feet. It vanished from his view. Unlocking the lap belt deactivated the automatic parachute opening apparatus built into the ejection seat. He fumbled with the ripcord for what seemed like an eternity. Finally, he felt it move. The chute unfurled with a loud snap. When the canopy opened, the riser cords and panels stretched beyond their tolerance requirements but held together. His torso was squeezed downward, as if it were in a vice. Fortunately, he was not injured. No spine injuries. No injuries to internal organs. His young age and physical condition played an important part in the outcome. Unfortunately, he opened the chute at about 30,000 feet. It would be close to an agonizing half hour and twenty miles over three counties before his shoes touched down on South Carolina soil.

Should evaluate to see if landing is possible, Howard pondered. *Better to determine the flying characteristics at high altitude in event it is un-*

successful . . . could get squirrelly, probably use up considerable amount of altitude in recovery attempt . . . or eject. He keyed the interphone and said, "I'm going to simulate a landing as close as possible. I have no idea how this beast will react, so be ready to eject if it should get out of control. I'm going to level off at 20,000 feet and slow to 220 indicated air speed." Reaching 20,000 and 220 knots, Howard transmitted, "Bob, let's start with 10 degrees of flap, then pause for a short time to see how she flies. If that works, continue lowering them in 10-degree increments. Advise before each movement."

"Rog, 10 degrees, now." Bob located the wing flap lever with his right hand, keeping his eyes on the wing flap indicator. He pulled up, then aft on the lever until the needle on the flap indicator reached 10 degrees, then immediately moved the lever to the OFF position. The crew felt a slight sensation of deceleration without any additional yaw, which indicated the flaps were functioning normally. Howard nudged the elevator forward ever so slightly and increased power to keep the indicated air speed on 220.

"Ivory 2, Hunter Tower. How do you read, over?"

"Better answer them, Bob. They may think we've crashed. Find out more about that runway construction."

"Roger," Bob replied. "Flaps coming down another ten degrees."

"Hunter Tower, Ivory 2 inbound to land from the northwest. Need all emergency equipment standing by. Provide more information on runway condition."

"Roger, Ivory 2. Fire fighting equipment and medical have been alerted. Construction is on the runway overruns only. However, use caution. There is an 18-inch drop-off at the beginning of the actual runway. The on-duty Operations Officer, who is B-47 qualified, is in the Tower for additional assistance. Also, we have all the field lighting set at maximum." Tower desired to keep the emergency frequency open for other possible uses and transmitted, "If feasible, switch to my frequency, 381.4, over."

Bob transmitted, "Roger," as he changed the radio frequency from 243.0 emergency to 381.4."

"Tower, Ivory 2 on 381.4."

"Ivory 2, Hunter Tower, loud and clear."

As Howard completed the flap evaluation, his mind was churning, evaluating the runway problem.

As if we don't have enough to worry about, they throw a runway problem at us. Don't want to risk flying all the way to Homestead. Gotta make this work.

"Okay, Bob, she seems fairly stable with full flaps. Lower the gear, but if you sense anything unusual, bring the gear back up immediately."

"Yes, sir. Gear down, now."

Howard pushed all five throttles slightly forward to compensate for the drag when the gear doors open and the gear begins to extend. The gear extended with a slight jar when it locked into the down position. The gear indicators at the pilot and co-pilot position indicated all four gears down and locked. Howard adjusted the throttles again to maintain 220 knots indicated.

After he experimented by making small turns and power adjustments, he transmitted, "I see no difference in the handling characteristics with the gear and flaps up or down. Your opinion, Bob?"

"Concur."

Howard thought for a moment, then transmitted. "Just before flare, it will be necessary to keep the right wing higher to prevent the number six engine from coming into contact with the surface. That's assuming it's still attached. That, of course, is a cross-control condition. Cross-control increases the descent rate. This technique is used by pilots if the aircraft is not equipped with flaps. However, a cross-control, if overdone, can result in a violent stall. I'm going to see if there are any problems using the cross-control." When he turned the control wheel, it stuck momentarily, then functioned normally. Howard removed some pressure off of the left rudder and the heading remained stable. He smiled for the first time in several minutes and transmitted, "I believe this will work. I removed almost all the left rudder and she flew straight ahead. Your thoughts, Bob?"

"I agree, Major. Incredibly, it seems the yaw to the right is cancelled by the slight aileron input."

"That's my thought exactly. Now I'm going to slowly decrease the speed to 200. If this is reasonably successful, I'll reduce the final approach speed to 200 just prior to the threshold. Again, if this machine seems to get out of control, let's eject immediately.

"Any comments or suggestions?"

Silence.

"Okay, here we go." Howard reduced power slowly and eased back on the control column to maintain altitude. The airspeed indicator needle crept backward . . . 212 knots, 208 knots. At 200 knots, Howard relaxed the elevator slightly and the Stratojet began a slow but unsteady descent. The vibrations were more pronounced than at 220 knots; otherwise, there was no significant change. Howard flew straight and level for a minute, then made some shallow turns.

"Looks like she will stay in the air at 200 knots. Now I'm going to give her the final and toughest test by raising the starboard wing about 12 degrees and maintain the current heading. Any questions?"

Silence.

Howard gently input left aileron until the right wing was high enough in his estimation to prevent the engine from striking the surface when landing. The aircraft shuddered as if on the verge of a stall. Howard kept the wing up for approximately 1 minute, the amount of time he estimated would be necessary when landing. Then he pushed the nose over, adding power to increase the speed to 220 knots.

Whew. Glad that's over. It's nerve-racking when delving into the unknown . . . especially with two other people depending on you for their safety.

"Okay, Bob, raise the gear. Once it's up and locked, raise the flaps in 10-degree increments."

"Roger."

After the gear and flaps were up, Howard transmitted, "Gentlemen, let's analyze our situation. I'll summarize what I know, and you add anything you think is significant or if you disagree, please say so. This is no time to be bashful. Forget about rank for the moment. Our lives are on the line. Tell me what you're thinking. We've got a severely bent, unstable aircraft. It takes almost three-fourths left rudder to hold a steady heading with wings level. The ailerons are not functioning normally. Left aileron snags about halfway through, and force is required to move beyond that point. Control of the aircraft is marginal at best. The runway is under construction, which will probably require a longer than normal touchdown point. The approach speed must be higher than normal. I want to use as much runway as feasible in case our hydraulics are inoperative, but if we land short, we're in big trouble because of the construction. We've got a big fat nuke as a passenger, and it would most likely career through the fuselage and explode if we land short and collide with the runway under repair. It's dark, and we're all fatigued. Three things I see in our favor are calm winds at the airdrome, the favorable cross-control, and our fuel is sufficient but not a weight problem for landing. All in all, not a pretty picture as I see it. Any ideas, comments, or suggestions?"

"I concur with your assessment," Bob replied. "When we get on final approach in thicker air, this aircraft may react differently, especially if you keep the starboard wing high on account of number six hanging down. If that engine should fall from the wing in that configuration, at a low altitude . . . it'd be difficult to avoid crashing. On the other hand, if number six drags when we land, it might cause us to swerve to the starboard and exit the runway. Stalling could be a problem if and when we drop below 200 knots. Should it stall, hopefully we'll be at a survivable altitude. We really don't know for sure the extent of the damage. Even so, I'm not too keen on ejecting. Not yet anyway. Will you use the brake chute?"

"Good points, Bob. Those factors should and will be considered. I plan to start the final approach with gear and flaps full down, indicating around 220 knots. About 30 knots faster than norm. I'll slow somewhat near the runway threshold. It's reasonably stable at 220 indicated air speed, but as you know, the vibrations increase substantially and she tends to wallow more as the speed decreases. And any speed below 200 knots is in the realm of the unknown. It's a trade-off between being too fast, run off the end of the runway . . . and too slow and lose control or stall. I don't think a go-around is an option we should consider. We've got to do it right the first time. After the airspeed drops below 220 knots, I want you to call out the speed each time it changes 5 knots and the altitude in 100-foot increments. As soon as the first wheel touches the runway, pull the brake chute."

"Wilco on the brake chute. How about a chase aircraft to look us over for damage?"

"Excellent. Work on that, Bob."

"Leland, your thoughts please."

"You both have pretty well summed up our predicament. We're in a world of hurt as I see it. I agree with Bob: I think we should eject only if necessary. If we dispense with that 7,600-pounder riding in the bomb bay, would that help stabilize and allow a slower speed on final approach?"

There was no response for almost a minute as the crew members contemplated the seriousness of ejecting a nuclear weapon. The idea of ditching the bomb had, at some point in time, briefly entered the thought process of the entire crew, only to be put aside. At least until now. This was a defining moment.

They're waiting for my answer, Howard thought. *I'm the one up here in the driver's seat. The one who must make the decision, and I wouldn't want it any other way regardless of the difficulty. My first priority is to protect my subordinates. Eliminating the weight and danger of explosion would help in that endeavor . . . I could drop it offshore, hopefully in a location that will assure reasonable expectations for recovery.*

Finally, Howard keyed his interphone mike and spoke.

"Good point, Leland. The thought of getting rid of that bomb has been in the back of my mind for some time. There are complications, however. As we all know, dumping a nuclear weapon in the ocean is a serious matter—certainly not to be taken lightly. Yes, it would make the aircraft more stable, allow a lower speed, and avoid the risk of an explosion if our landing is . . . unsuccessful. SAC Tactical Doctrine dictates that crew safety is paramount over all other considerations."

Howard scanned the instruments and continued a slow descent, maintaining 220 knots while he hashed out all the details and pondered his situation. The other two crewmembers were anxiously awaiting a decision, and he knew it. As the aircraft commander, the final decision was his alone. The pressure was on. His left foot and leg ached from the constant rudder pressure required to prevent the aircraft from turning. The strobe of the rotating beacon located on top of the Hunter Control Tower flashed by.

Howard had a flashback to World War II during a mission to bomb Munich in a B-17G, *The Mississippi Miss.* An hour northwest of Munich, the sky suddenly blossomed with Me-109s. They approached from above, hidden in the sun, pouncing on the formation from all directions, a few head-on. Although a tight formation was maintained, several of the Flying Fortresses were hit and exploded, which damaged other aircraft in the close formation. Others lost power, descended, and were chewed to pieces by the Luftwaffe who loved to prey on the semi-helpless. Some parachutes were observed but not enough to cover all the crewmembers. One of the Me-109s raked *The Mississippi Miss* but only damaged the aircraft skin. Near the target, the fighters disappeared to avoid the flak, which was so thick it appeared as if you could walk on it.

After the bombs were dropped and the flak subsided, they were pounced on by a new set of fighters. *The Mississippi Miss* took her share of hits, but again no crew members were injured or killed, and the Fortress miraculously managed to survive and fight another day. Many others were not so fortunate. By overcoming great apprehension and fear that day in July 1944, he had managed to keep his composure as the aircraft commander and return his crew safely to England. Now was the appropriate time and circumstance to repeat that performance. He could and would.

After two agonizing minutes with his mind in a whirlwind, he thumbed the mike and announced, "Bob, tell the tower to get authorization from Omaha to jettison the weapon off-shore. Determine whether they have an aircraft that is available for damage assessment and, if so, when it can be airborne. Tell Operations to apprise Homestead of our situation."

CHAPTER SEVENTEEN

The pilot of Pug Gold 2 glanced at his watch, illuminated by the bright moonlight, and calculated that he had been descending for approximately twelve minutes. His entire body was in pain because of the stress of the collision, ejecting, deceleration, and the extreme cold temperature. Remnants of the Sabre rested on the surface except for some light pieces of insulation and paper documents from the cockpit, which fluttered slowly earthward. The major parts, including the fuselage, lay in a plowed field six miles south of a small town called Sylvania, Georgia. The 24 MK 4 Mighty Mouse rockets lay nearby.

He was not cognizant of the fact that strong upper winds had silently carried him twelve miles overland to the Savannah River since he'd ejected near Sylvania. Several miles of swamp extended outward from both sides of the river, which was teeming with alligators and snakes. Not a convenient place to land. But as fate would dictate and smile upon him, his current altitude was 15,000 feet, which was sufficient to carry him well east of the swamp.

Pug Gold 3 departed the area because of low fuel, heading for Charleston. The pilot of Pug Gold 2 was on his own, descending silently in his parachute. It was dark below, except for the faint lights of two tugboats slowly struggling upriver. He wondered what fate had in store, and how he'd gotten into such a fix. Did the B-47 survive the collision? He might be faced with a court martial. Kicked out of the Air Force. What would his family think? His Air Force buddies? His Mississippi neighbors? Was the collision his fault? He tried to put these negative thoughts out of his mind. Concentrate on the present. Survival was much more important than a career or what some busybody might infer.

He wished he had been more prudent in selecting his clothing and had kept his gloves on. He was thankful for the helmet and face mask, which provided some protection from the extreme temperature. He wished the bright moonlight could provide some warmth. Perhaps it would be useful in selecting a landing spot. He pondered whether he would be able to grasp and pull the parachute risers for directional control. If not, he would be along for the ride and land where the wind and gravity sent him.

When Bob forwarded the request for an escort aircraft and authorization to eject the bomb offshore, Hunter AFB jumped with activity. The Operations Officer, Major John Wilshire, hurried down the metal stairs to a room below the control tower cab with a small radio in his hand. He unlocked a steel reinforced door to a room marked "Restricted Entry Authorized Personnel Only," flipped the light switch on, and locked the door. He approached a large safe located in a corner of the room. From memory, he spun a round dial several times in different directions, pulled the heavy door open by its handle, and snatched a booklet annotated "Authentication Codes TOP SECRET." He hurriedly flipped the pages to February 5, 1958, then picked up a red phone labeled OFF HDQTRS. A secure, direct line was automatically connected from the control tower through base operations to SAC Headquarters, Offutt AFB, in Omaha, Nebraska.

Deep inside the bowels of the bomb-proof building at Offutt, the on-duty assistant operations officer, Colonel Winfred Boduski, glanced at his elaborate communications panel to see where the call originated. A somewhat agitated Boduski had reported for duty at 11 PM and was hoping for a quiet mid-shift. A call from a base this time of night on the red secure phone couldn't bode good news. He cleared his voice, punched the flashing button, and picked up the phone.

"SAC Headquarters, Colonel Boduski. Authenticate please."

After Wilshire stated the correct series of numbers and letters, Colonel Boduski accepted the call.

"Go ahead, Hunter."

"Colonel Boduski, Major Wilshire, Operations Officer, Hunter. We have a situation here, sir."

"Go on."

We're in communication with a B-47B, call sign Ivory 2. The aircraft commander says they were involved in a mid-air collision, has severe damage, and intends to land here. He requests permission to jettison his payload offshore in the Atlantic."

"What type of payload?"

"He didn't give the nomenclature. I assume he's carrying some sort of nuclear weapon."

"Major, we can't assume anything in this business," Colonel Boduski shot back in an antagonizing manner.

"Yes, sir. I agree, sir. He wants to lighten his payload in order to reduce his speed on final approach and eliminate the possibility of an explosion on or near the base in case he crashes."

"What's the location of this aircraft, Ivory 2?"

"ETA at Hunter in about five minutes. He was northwest of the field when he initially called the tower. Do you want me to ask the pilot what type of weapon he wants to jettison?"

"Negative," said Colonel Boduski. "Stand by while I determine what type of bomb he has onboard."

The colonel typed "Ivory 2" on his computer keyboard, and the entire flight plan and all the details of the flight—including the bombing score—appeared on a screen. A printer began printing a hardcopy.

As the colonel reviewed the details of Major Richardson's flight plan, he thought to himself, *Hmm. Major Howard Richardson's cargo is a Mark 15 Mod Zero thermonuclear bomb. Holy smoke. He's asking approval for a Broken Arrow!*

"Stand by on this line, Major."

"Wilco, Colonel."

The pilot of Pug Gold 2 anxiously looked around for some sign of life on the surface. He reasoned that he should be on the ground, or nearly so. The last sign of civilization had been the lights of a house and a vehicle several minutes ago. Although a house was located nearby, the lights were out, and he did not see it as he neared the ground. At about 100 yards above the ground, he recognized a gravel road, trees, and other objects. The ground appeared to be coming up quickly to meet him. Remembering the ejection procedures, he moved his legs together and slightly bent them at the knees in anticipation of hitting the ground. According to his training manual, he was supposed to keep his head up and look at the horizon. That suggestion didn't material-ize. He looked down, raised his arms, and tried with all his strength to grasp the front risers to control and slow his descent rate, but his fingers refused to cooperate. Whoomp! His toes touched soil almost 23 miles east of where the collision occurred. He twisted and fell on his right side in an attempt to distribute some of the shock to his body and protect his legs. The temperature was 35 degrees, much warmer than where he'd ejected but not enough to thaw his hands.

His parachute canopy fluttered to the ground. He laid on his side for a short time, then slowly sat upright, crossed his legs, and gazed at his surroundings. It was very quiet except for the occasional bark of a dog somewhere off in the distance. No insects chirping. No aircraft droning overhead. No vehicle lights. Only an occasional, silent shoot-ing star and that barking dog.

He made a quick assessment of his limbs and extremities. His right side ached from the landing, but everything seemed to be connected and usable except for his hands. He decided the best option was to stay put at least until daylight. He glanced at his wrist watch again. 1:06 AM. A long time to wait for the warm rays of the sun. His body shivered. He pulled the parachute canopy toward him with excruciating pain and wrapped the canopy around his body, then placed the dinghy over his helmet for additional protection. He pushed his stiff hands under his armpits and waited. Although he was not aware of it, he was fortunate in that he could have landed in a clump of nearby trees, a barb-wire fence, or a swamp.

CHAPTER EIGHTEEN

hen Ivory 2 passed over Hunter AFB, Bob transmitted, "Ivory 2 over Hunter, 10,000 feet, slow descent, eastbound." The controllers craned their necks looking for the crippled B-47B. They informed Ivory 2 that a T-33 was available, but it would be almost an hour before a crew could be called in and become airborne. Howard informed them to forget the chase aircraft but to continue prodding SAC referencing his request.

Another five minutes went by without any word from Omaha. Howard impatiently thumbed his interphone and stated, "Gentleman, if SAC doesn't give us the nod, I'll make the decision in about ten minutes. In any case, we're going to jettison our cargo with or without headquarter approval in accordance with SAC Tactical Doctrine. Leland, tweak your radar as best you can. Take several photographs of the radar screen: before the bomb is released, at the time of release, and one or two afterward. At actual drop time, jot down the lat/long, altitude, heading, aircraft speed, time, and upper wind data. Hopefully they will be able to locate and recover the bomb—if it doesn't explode on contact with the water."

"Roger, sir. The radar is functioning normally. I can clearly see the outline of the coastline. I'll copy all the data you requested and make several photographs of the radar."

"Okay, Leland, and thanks." Howard scanned his instrument panel, continuing eastbound in a slow descent, leaving 9,500 feet at 220 knots indicated air speed.

Howard keyed his mike again. "Bob, if you're not busy at drop time, record our heading, altitude, airspeed, and outside temperature as a back-up and comparison to Leland's data. After the bomb is released and I turn westbound toward Hunter, start the same procedure we used earlier to lower the flaps and gear. Announce each time just before taking any action. And remember to pull the brake chute as we discussed."

"Wilco, Major."

"And Bob, in addition to the speed and altitude advisories, please keep an eye on your instruments during final approach. Let me know immediately if you don't like what you see or sense."

"Roger."

"We're passing the shoreline," Leland announced.

Howard gazed out the left side of the canopy. He visualized the shoreline fairly accurately using the surface lights along the shoreline.

"Roger, Leland. How much longer til you're ready to drop?"

"Estimate five minutes."

Howard glanced at the clock on his instrument panel. 1:06 AM. He started a gentle right turn, added some power, and leveled at 7,000 feet.

"Leland, let's drop as soon as you're ready and we're clear of the coast and any surface contacts. I'm at 7,000 feet and will maintain that altitude until the drop."

Yes, sir."

"And Leland, take your time. We've got adequate fuel. Make sure everything is covered. What we're about to do will be scrutinized for months, possibly years to come. They'll nit-pick every detail. Let's do it right."

Leland looked at the Bomb Control Panel and replied, "Wilco, Major Richardson."

Just as Howard completed his second orbit in the holding pattern, Leland advised, "Drop Checklist complete. Suggest continue right turn to 090. I see no surface contacts. I'll manually release the weapon when well clear of land."

"Roger, right to 090 heading."

Leland moved the Bomb Door and Release Control Switch to the MANUAL position and moved the door switch to OPEN. The wounded Stratojet shuddered as the spoiler and bomb bay doors opened. Howard added a bit of power to compensate for the increased drag.

The Bomb Door Indicator confirmed the doors were open and Leland announced, "Bomb bay doors open."

Seconds later, Leland checked his radar screen. This was the first time he had actually released a nuclear weapon. At Radford and at many other locations, he had transmitted an electronic signal, not a real bomb. But this was different. Very different. His trembling finger touched the spring-loaded Drop Control Switch. He paused, bowed his head for a short interval, toggled the switch to the FREE position, and held it until he felt the aircraft jump upward when the Stratojet was relieved of its burden.

At 1:14 AM, Leland stepped on his transmitter key and announced, "Bomb away." He snapped a photograph of the radar screen, closed the doors, and started collecting other data. Shortly after the bomb cleared the aircraft, two parachutes automatically unfurled, slowing its descent rate and providing extra time for Howard to escape the drop zone.

Howard glanced at the red glow of the Bomb Away Indicator Light on his instrument panel, reduced power, and started a right turn and slow descent from 7,000 feet toward Hunter.

"Flaps coming down ten degrees," Bob transmitted. "Before Landing Checklist when you're ready, sir."

"Roger, advise the tower we're inbound for straight into runway 27 and have all emergency equipment standing by. Then go ahead with the checklist."

When Bob called the Control Tower, he was advised that SAC had just approved jettisoning the bomb twenty miles offshore.

Bob continued the checklist. After the flaps were fully down, he transmitted, "Extending gear."

Bomb should be in the drink by now, Howard reasoned. *Didn't see a flash or feel a concussion. Guess it didn't explode.*

The crew felt a slight jar when the gear lowered. Immediately, both of the pilots did a double-take when they looked at the Landing Gear Indicator. The tab for the aft main gear was in an up position. A red light illuminated on the gear lever at both pilot positions, which confirmed their predicament.

What next? Howard thought. *The gear was okay less than an hour ago . . . What changed? Just five days ago, an aft wheel collapsed on a B-47 during take-off . . . tail struck the runway . . . aircraft broke in two, spilled fuel, terrible fire. All killed.*

He realized that he was gripping the yoke tightly with his left hand. He removed his hand from the yoke, slowly unfurled his tingling fingers, and rubbed them against his leg. *Relax. Get a grip on yourself.*

Concentrate. You've got a tough job to do. Do it and do it right. That gear must come down or else . . .

"Bob, I'll complete the checklist. Use the ELGE and try to get that gear down ASAP."

Bob transmitted, "Roger," as he turned his seat to face backwards where the Emergency Landing Gear Extension controls were located. An Unsafe To Land red light glowed on the ELGE. Bob transmitted, "ELGE confirms unsafe to land. Major, please move the gear handle to the off position."

"Gear lever in OFF position, now."

As Howard uttered these words, the Mark 15 Mod 0 thermonuclear bomb struck the water near Tybee Island. There was no time for a checklist, but Howard recalled that the speed should not be above 200 knots indicated airspeed when using the ELGE.

"Bob, we're supposed to be at 200 or less, but obviously I can't go that slow at present time." He reduced the power slightly and said, "But I'll slow as much as safety permits."

Bob acknowledged the information, paused for a minute while the speed bled off, then pulled the ELGE lever labeled REAR. Small beads of perspiration formed on his forehead, and his armpits were soaked. His head and heart throbbed. Time was running out. He recalled Howard stating that a go-around would not be an option. He wondered what would happen if they were forced to land with the gear up. *Probably lose control and leave the runway.* He returned the lever to the upright position. It seemed like an eternity but in fact was only a few seconds when the uplocks released and the gear free-fell into position. He continued the process by vigorously moving the lever with full strokes, fore and aft.

The bright flashing approach and runway lights were clearly visible in the distance.

Howard constantly made adjustments with the rudder and ailerons as he fought to maintain a constant heading and remain lined up with the runway. He estimated he was five miles from the runway. Altitude 1,700 feet, speed 208 knots.

"I'll start the cross-control and reduce speed after I leave 500 feet." He glanced at the Landing Gear Indicator. The tab indicated the gear was still up.

"Bob, gear status."

"Still pumping. No green light and no extra resistance."

"Roger."

"Make sure you're strapped in tight. If I get us safely on the ground, let's abandon as soon as safety permits."

The flashing lights from emergency vehicles mixed with the runway lights cast an eerie glow. The wounded Stratojet tried to wallow back and forth as if it didn't want to land, but Howard corrected each movement before it became a problem.

Five hundred feet, 199 knots.

Howard's eyes flitted back and forth from the instrument panel to the runway, but speed and altitude information were not forthcoming. The instruments were unreadable due to the extreme vibration. From now on, he would fly by the "seat-of-his-pants."

"I'll hold her tail off the runway as long as possible. Be prepared for a hard landing and possible break-up."

I may have damaged the ratchet pawls and jammed the gear because of the excessive speed, Howard thought.

Two hundred feet, 195 knots.

One hundred feet, 190 knots.

Bob felt resistance when he moved the lever. A green light illuminated on the ELGE and at both pilot positions. "Gear down and locked," Bob transmitted, excited. He returned his seat to face forward.

The wounded Stratojet shimmied.

Over the threshold, 90 feet, slightly left of centerline, 184 knots, violent vibrations, yawing and weaving to the extreme. Howard caressed the controls that he knew so well. Rudder, aileron, elevator, power. Clear of the construction. He kept his eyes glued on the runway. The crucial time had come. He turned the control column left and raised the right wing.

All eyes in the control tower intently observed the approach, some with binoculars, some with their fingers crossed. He kept the right wing up and continued straight ahead for a few seconds, eased back on the elevator, and started a flare. She floated. Lights flashed by in his peripheral vision. He pulled all five throttles to idle. She floated. *Drifting farther left. Come on, baby. Get down. Get down.* Crunch! The tires screamed and spewed smoke. The Stratojet bounced and became airborne for a few seconds, then settled to the runway, well left of center-line and almost off the runway. When the wheels touched the runway the second time, at 1:26 AM, Bob yanked on the brake chute handle. Howard stood on the brake pedals. The brake chute unfurled as adver-tised, and Ivory 2 slowed enough to allow a turnoff at the last taxiway.

When the Stratojet cleared the runway, Howard's hands went into automatic control; he flipped the canopy switch to "RAISE," moved all five throttles to CUTOFF, and set the parking brake. He exhaled a sigh of relief. "Let's get out of this crate, now." Everyone in the Tower jumped with excitement. Leland didn't hear Howard's last command. He had unbuckled as soon as the turnoff began, opened the exit door, and pressed the knob to lower the ladder. Bob was close behind Leland, followed by Howard holding his family photograph in one hand. They scampered down the ladder, bent down, and kissed the tarmac.

EPILOGUE

After the firefighters declared the crippled B47B safe, the medics, firefighters, and operations personnel gathered around Howard and his crew with loud applause and many congratulations on a job well done. The hour was late, and after some standard forms were completed in operations, the exhausted men were driven to the Visiting Officers Quarters in a blue Air Force sedan.

On the way, Howard suggested they jot down every detail they could recall before retiring. He reminded them, in a hushed voice, that he was once assigned to SAC Headquarters and was familiar with the many questions and answers required by crew members involved in an accident. They would most likely be required to meet a Court Martial Board, who would consider them guilty unless they could prove otherwise.

He spent almost an hour at a desk making notes on VOQ stationary. When he was finished, he climbed in bed and finally dozed off in a restless sleep. Soon afterward, at 5:00 AM, his phone rang. Major Wilshire, the Operation Officer, informed him that General Thomas S. Power, Commander-in-Chief of SAC, was en route from Homestead—ETA in approximately thirty minutes—to inspect the damaged aircraft and receive a briefing by the aircraft commander. General Power was visiting Homestead to observe the USCM.

Howard asked Major Wilshire to inform Bob and Leland and provide transportation to base operations.

There was no time to shower, and besides, he didn't have a change of clothes. So he splashed cold water on his face, ignored the heavy twenty-hour stubble, ran his fingers through his thick black hair, and dressed. He felt grungy. Not the ideal way to meet the top dog of SAC.

At the base operations briefing room, the three huddled around a desk in a corner and compared notes.

The room buzzed with excitement and activity when word spread that Power was inbound. All three crew members' notes were essentially the same. A few minor changes were made, upon which all three agreed. A high altitude jet navigation chart was taped to an easel. Leland drew the route of flight in black up to the point of collision and red thereafter. Local and Zulu time was depicted at each checkpoint. Howard rehearsed his presentation to Bob and Leland using a pointer to emphasize key points. A few adjustments were made, tweaked again.

Upon arrival, General Power inspected the damaged B-47B. He was amazed that Howard and his crew had been able to make a successful landing. When General Power and his entourage of generals and a colonel entered operations, everyone snapped to attention when the base commander called "Attention." Power was dressed in a flight suit without his four stars on his shoulders, but he stood out prominently to everyone in the room. Power called "At ease" as he strode over to Howard and introduced himself and his staff. Howard introduced Bob and Leland. After some small talk, Power was seated, and Howard began his briefing.

The general had been given a full briefing about all three crew members while en route to Hunter. He was impressed with their spotless records, especially Howard's thirty-five combat missions during the war. He also noted that their earlier practice bomb run over Radford had been rated a perfect score. Power didn't interrupt Howard during the briefing but asked several relevant questions afterwards, which Howard answered to Power's satisfaction.

General Power thanked him and told him and his crew to gather their gear and fly back to Homestead with him. Howard felt a great sense of relief. He was exonerated. He could forget the Court Martial Board.

En route to Homestead, General Power visited with Howard. He had talked to General LeMay in Washington and recommended a medal for their superior airmanship.

On a sunny day, fitting for such an important occasion, Howard was awarded the Distinguished Flying Cross by General John McConnell, commander of the 2ⁿᵈ Air Force. The Air Force Commendation medal was awarded to Leland and Bob. Homestead marked the occasion with military parades, fly-bys, speeches by military leaders, and local dignitaries. Proud family members admired them from the decorated stands.

Howard was selected for membership into SAC's elite Heads Up Flying Club for his "skill, courage, and keen presence of mind in concern for the safety of others." Soon afterward, he became the Commanding Officer of a B-47B squadron, and his career spiraled upward. He completed tours in the Pentagon, Germany, and graduated from the Air Command and Staff School at Maxwell Air Force Base. Along the way, he flew B-52s, obtained an MBA, was promoted twice, and perhaps ironically, became the Commanding Officer of the Nuclear Weapons School. Howard retired as a full colonel after thirty-one years of commendable service.

He currently resides in Brandon, Mississippi with his gracious wife Vivian, just a few short miles from their birthplace. He maintains an active lifestyle and enjoys reminiscing about *The Mississippi Miss*, B-47s, B-52s, Reflex missions, and the Broken Arrow incident. He is a proud member of the Quiet Birdmen and the B-47 Association. The international media interest level still remains high concerning the bomb and his exploits.

At first, the Air Force declared the aircraft as being "economically repairable" but reversed its decision after further evaluation. The B-47B was scrapped and never flew again.

Robert J. Lagerstrom left the Air Force after his commitment was over. He joined American Airlines just as the jet-age was emerging, when passengers were treated like royalty and pilots were put on an even higher pedestal. He was a proud member and past President of the Grey Eagles, member of the Quiet Birdmen, and member of the Silver Stripes. He had a wonderful, safe, and illustrious career with a great company. Ironically and sadly, Mr. Lagerstrom passed away on February 5, 2009, the 51st anniversary of the Broken Arrow accident.

The pilot of Pug Gold 2 was found by a local resident just before daylight because of the persistent barking of his dog. After receiving medical treatment at a local hospital, he was flown back to Charleston in a helicopter. He spent several days recovering from his injuries, primarily to his fingers due to frostbite. He was exonerated after the aircraft Nadar unit was found several days after the accident, still attached to the canopy. The Nadar had recorded the radar presentation during the intercept. It proved that the radar in his F-86L malfunctioned, similar to the way it had malfunctioned the day before the accident. Another pilot flew the aircraft the previous day and made the following write-up: "Radar inoperative. No Phase II or III." The official records do not indicate any action was taken to correct the radar problem before the accident.

He remained in the Air Force and flew combat missions over Vietnam. He retired after an illustrious career and resides in northern Florida.

Edgar R Armagost held several important positions in the Air Force after his command of the 792nd. His last position was at the FAA Headquarters in Washington as a Liaison Officer. He retired as a Lieutenant Colonel and resides in Northern Florida.

When a Broken Arrow is declared, the military moves swiftly. A tremendous effort to find the lost bomb got underway on short notice. Hunter AFB was the staging ground for the search, which began the following day on February 6. Although a plutonium capsule necessary for a nuclear explosion was not in the bomb, it did contain 400 pounds of high explosive and a substantial amount of uranium. The following letter describes the great hunt in detail.

Airmunitions Letter, Headquarters, Ogden Air Material Area, United States Air Force, Hill Air Force Base, Utah, 23 June 1960, OOAMA, Airmunitions Ltr. No. 136-11-56A, Page 7 (Declassified from "Secret Restricted Data Atomic Energy Act 1954")

A B-47 Aircraft jettisoned a (Deleted) weapon off the coast of Georgia and fixed an approximate position of impact for subsequent recovery. Being underwater recovery the U. S. Navy had priority for the recovery operation with the USAF EOD acting as liaison at the scene. EOD personnel coordinated in the search efforts to include land search of the beach area adjacent to the computed impact area, underwater visual search and underwater hand-held sonar gear. Helicopter reconnaissance was also employed with negative results. The Navy employed a Submarine Rescue Ship, Mine Sweeper (with SONAR gear), a U. S. Coast Guard Cutter, two fifteen foot boats with outboard motors, a second Mine Sweeper with sweeping gear, high speed troop transports, a 1000 ton barge, a Catamaran, and LCVP and an LCP in the search efforts. Final reports were submitted on this incident in April 1958 with negative results. All efforts had been expended that was considered feasible with no actual positive contact made with the weapon or any of its components throughout the search. Item was assumed to have been completely buried under many feet of mud bottom or to have disintegrated upon impact. In either situation search was abandoned and case was closed. (There were no photos.)

Unusual problems: The weapon was not recovered. Pinpoint impact was not provided. Expert Photo-Radar Interpretation of the "scope pictures" immediately proceeding, during and following the actual drop was not accomplished. A recommendation was made that a dye-marker be incorporated into the after-body of nuclear weapons for the purpose of possible recovery in a situation of this type.

Contamination: None registered.

Although it was during a busy and critical time, diligent effort was expended by the flight crew to take several photographs of the radar—one shot at the instant of jettison, to be used for recovery purposes. The above letter confirms that the photographs were taken; but for unknown reasons, they were not properly utilized by the search officials. Apparently, the latitude and longitude at time of jettison were used. If the photographs of the radar had been scrutinized by a panel of experts, a very precise impact zone most likely could have been established rather than the three square mile area that was searched. The photographs depicted the exact position of the aircraft at time of jettison in relation to the shoreline and islands in the immediate area. Coupled with this information and data from the aircraft, such as heading, altitude, speed, and upper winds, the search outcome may have been entirely different. If the photographs still exist, perhaps another review should be made by appropriate authority to determine whether the search was made in the correct area.

If the high explosives in the bomb didn't explode on contact with the surface, the bomb still resides somewhere near Tybee Island, most likely under several feet of silt and mud. The controversy rages on about the disposition of the bomb. In 2000, Congressman Jack Kingston (R-GA) requested the Air Force reinvestigate the accident following inquiries from constituents and the media. The Air Force consulted the Navy, Department of Energy, Savannah District Army Corps of Engineers, and the Skidaway Oceanographic Institute to investigate the details surrounding the incident, the most likely current condition of the bomb, associated hazards, and to determine whether search and subsequent recovery operations should be attempted. As a result, The Air Force Nuclear Weapons and Counterproliferation Agency recommended that the bomb remain undisturbed and continue to be categorized as irretrievably lost for the following reasons: No possibility of a nuclear explosion. No risk to the public. Avoids potential for unacceptable impact to the environment, including potential damage to the Floridian aquifer.

The Air Force considered the case to be closed until July 2004, when media reports indicated a citizens group had detected enhanced levels of radiation in Wassaw Sound.

The Air Force assembled a group of experts from three government agencies, plus representatives from the citizens group, to investigate and hopefully quell the uproar. The investigation determined that the radiation was from naturally occurring minerals and not the lost Mk-15 bomb.

If anything favorable about this incident can be said, it would be in regards to the collision impact point. The B-47B wing is substantially reinforced or "hardened" at the impact location to support the wing fuel tank, which carries over 11,000 pounds of jet fuel. If the wing had been struck on either side of this hardened area, it most certainly would have separated from the aircraft. If so, the B-47B would have become uncontrollable. The left wing would produce more lift than the right stub and the right engine would be missing, resulting in a violent clockwise roll of a magnitude severe enough to require immediate crew ejection.

Fate, circumstance, timing, and destiny are strange bedfellows. Was this accident pre-ordained? Fortunately, it's quite difficult for two aircraft to meet at a precise time in a three dimensional sky. Numerous variables would have prevented the two aircraft from colliding. For instance, if the radar in the F-86L Sabre had been repaired, the accident probably would not have occurred. If either aircraft had been at a slightly different altitude, theoretically the collision would not have happened. If either aircraft had changed their heading, even slightly, the collision may not have occurred. If either aircraft had changed power setting to increase or decrease speed, the accident may not have happened. If the GCI Director had issued different speeds or headings, the accident may not have happened. If either aircraft had aborted the mission for any of numerous reasons, the accident would not have occurred. But the accident did occur. Were the circumstances that brought these two aircraft and the four crew members together on this cold night in 1958 pre-ordained? Only you, the reader can make that determination.

ACKNOWLEDGMENTS

COLONEL HOWARD TRIPLETT RICHARDSON (USAF Ret) was the Aircraft Commander of Ivory 2, the B-47B entangled in this harrowing incident. Colonel Richardson spent many hours with me on the phone, answering my e-mails, reviewing, and making suggestions regarding the manuscript. I had the privilege of visiting him at his home where I relentlessly quizzed him on all aspects of his heroic flight. His knowledge of the B-47B bomber, the Strategic Air Command procedures, policies, and real life issues are beyond comparison. Without the input and guidance from this quiet-mannered southern gentleman, this book would lack much of its realism and gut-wrenching action. His gracious wife, Vivian Ann, provided details of their family life during their many years serving America. I hold Colonel Richardson at the highest level of esteem. He is a true American Hero, and I sincerely hope that my efforts to depict him in this light have been successful.

LIEUTENANT COLONEL EDGAR R. ARMAGOST (USAF Ret), Commanding Officer of the 792nd Aircraft Control and Warning Squadron, North Charleston, South Carolina, was on duty when the incident occurred and provided first-hand information on the control room atmosphere. He was generous in advising me on other technical aspects of the Air Defense Command. He was my commanding officer when I served at the 792nd AC&W Squadron. Lieutenant Colonel Armagost was a well-respected and admired commanding officer.

MAJOR RAYMOND G. BRONK (USAF Ret), an F-86L fighter pilot who provided technical information and flight characteristics of the F-86L. His expertise and insight provided a poignant look at the cold war era in which the Air Defense Command trained daily for a Russian attack that, fortunately, never happened. His recall of minute details concerning the F-86L is remarkable. Major Bronk (First Lieutenant at the time) was based at the 444th Fighter Interceptor Squadron, Charleston, S.C., when this incident happened. He was in the Charleston Naval Hospital when this incident occurred because of a mid-air collision in which he was involved the previous day with another F-86L.

PATRICK TILLERY, former Marine Corps pilot, FAA Center Controller, and editor of *Kilroy Was Here* was instrumental in obtaining vital information used in this book through his website, www. KilroyWasHere.org.

ROBERT IRWIN, Civil Servant at Charleston, South Carolina Air Force Base, assisted in locating Charleston-based 1958 era fighter pilots. Without the technical data, humor, and real-life experiences from the pilots, this book would be lacking much of its authenticity.

Thanks to the Air Force Safety Center for providing a copy of the Air-craft Mishap Report upon which this novel is based.

Excerpts from the U.S.-Soviet Arms Control and Disarmament meeting, courtesy of The Center for Defense Information.

Technical data about the B-47B was extracted from the USAF Flight Handbook.

IMAGES

The Mississippi Miss somewhere over Germany with several other Flying Fortresses in the background.

- Courtesy Colonel Howard T. Richardson (USAF Ret)

Busy airmen and officers in the 792nd AC&W Squadron, radar room known as Hemingway. The two airmen behind the large plexiglass board are aircraft plotters.

- Courtesy 1608th Air Transport Wing (M)
Charleston A.F.B. 1957

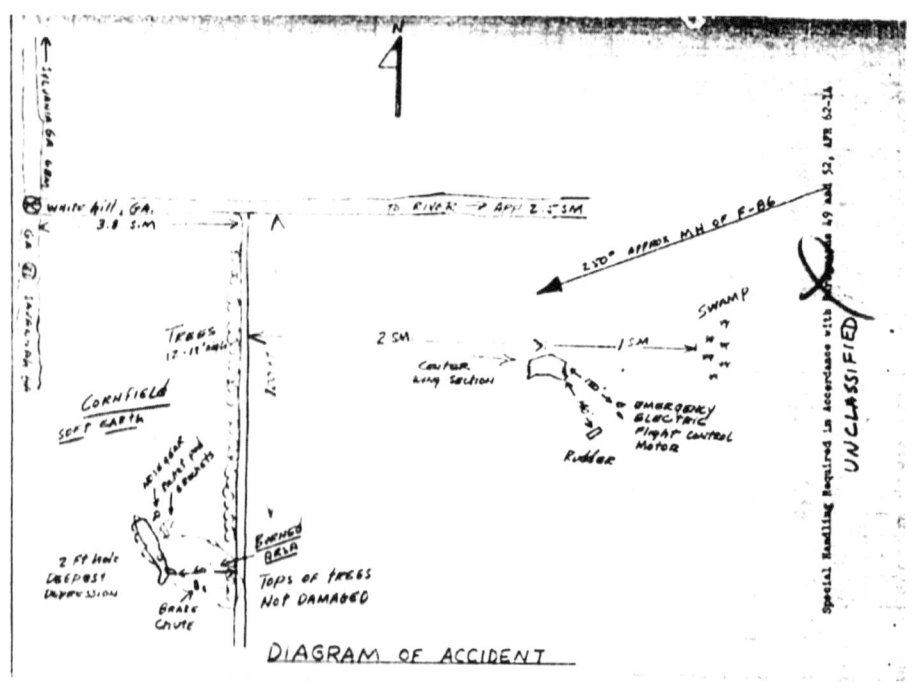

Location of the F-86L fuselage and scattered debris.
- Courtesy USAF Accident Board

A section of the F-86L port wing struck the aft starboard portion of the fuselage and vertical stabilizer. The starboard horizontal stabilizer was struck from the front by a heavy object - either a portion of the F-86L port wing or the wing center section.

- Courtesy USAF Accident Board

Section of outboard leading edge of the F-86L wing found in the B-47B
vertical stabilizer, jammed against the rudder post.

- Courtesy USAF Accident Board

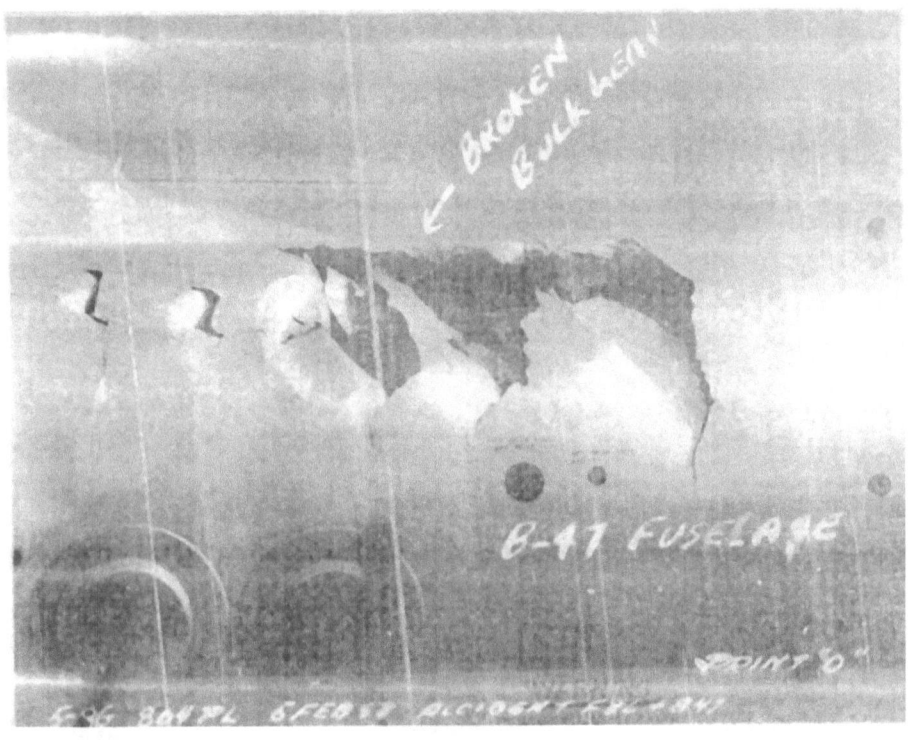

Close-up of the damaged B-47B fuselage.

- Courtesy USAF Accident Board

Number six engine hangs precariously from the front mount after the F-86L broke the rear mount.

- Courtesy USAF Accident Board

Close-up of the damage to the starboard wing of the B-47B on initial
contact by the F-86L.

This is the right auxiliary fuel tank torn from the B-47B.
- Courtesy of Colonel Howard T. Richardson (USAF Ret)

Damaged instrument panel from Pug Gold 2. Altimeter was set on 30.15. The Charleston altimeter was 30.19. If Pug Gold 1 was using 30.19 and Ivory 2 was using 29.92, that would explain the altitude difference when Pug Gold 1 informed Hemingway, "He is about angels 35.5."

- Courtesy USAF Accident Board

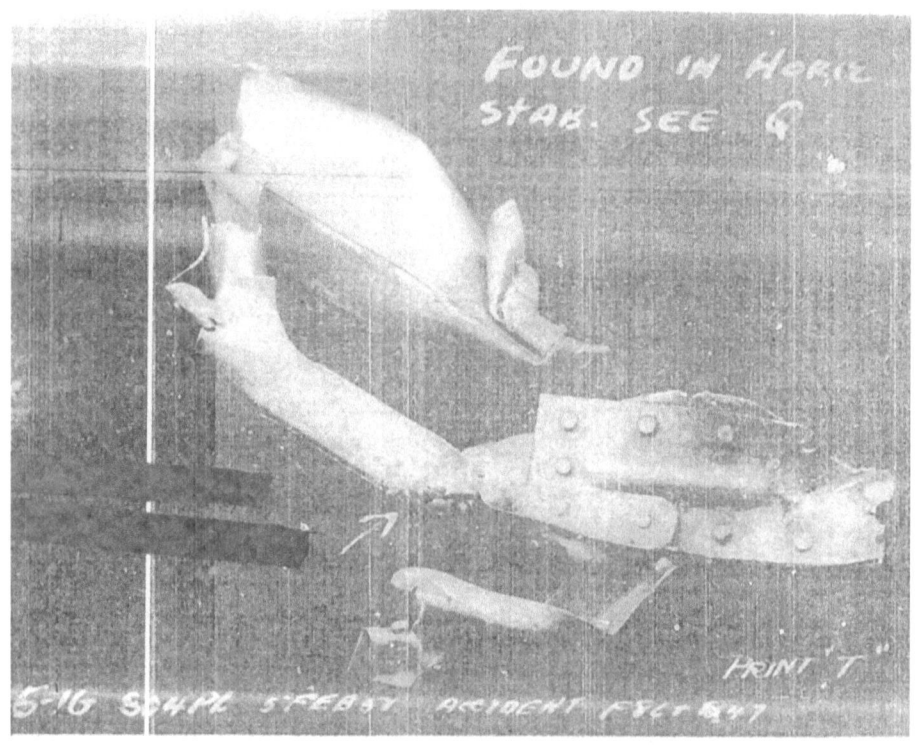

Piece of the F-86L found in the B-47B starboard horizontal stabilizer.
- Courtesy USAF Accident Board

Piece of the F-86L located in starboard wing of B-47B.
- Courtesy USAF Accident Board

THE FOLLOWING CERTIFIED FLYING TIME WAS EXTRACTED FROM THE OFFICIAL FORM 5 OF
HOWARD RICHARDSON AND WAS ACCOMPLISHED WITH THE U.S. ARMY AIR CORPS, 8th AIR
FORCE, 8th BOMBER COMMAND, 4th BOMBARDMENT WING, 385th BOMBARDMENT GROUP,
548th BOMBARDMENT SQUADRON, APO 559, USAAF, 155.

Year Month & Day	Aircraft Type Model & Series	FLYING TIME		TARGET
		DAY	NIGHT	
1944				
12 May	B-17 G	8:45		Zwichau
13 May	"	7:00		Osnobruck
19 May	"	9:45		Berlin
23 May	"	8:40		Chaumont
24 May	"	9:00		Berlin
25 May	"	7:00		Leige
27 May	"	8:00		Karlsruhe
28 May	"	9:00		Kontgsborn
29 May	"	8:20		Leipzig
31 May	"	7:30		Hamm
5 June	"	5:00		French Coast
6 June	"	6:30		Caen (D-Day)
6 June	"	4:30	2:00	Argetan (D-Day)
8 June	"	8:00		Nantes
11 June	"	5:30		Le Touquet
12 June	"	7:00		Montdidier
14 June	"	5:30	1:00	Florrennes
18 June	"	8:00		Hanover
21 June	"	10:00		Berlin
24 June	"	7:00		Wessermunde
6 July	"	4:15		Creppy
7 July	"	8:45		Merseburg
8 July	"	5:00	1:00	Conches
11 July	"	10:00		Munich
12 July	"	9:45		Munich
13 July	"	10:00		Munich
19 July	"	8:00		Edlesbach
20 July	"	8:30		Merseburg
21 July	"	8:45		Regensburg
24 July	"	5:45		Ground Support
25 July	"	6:00		Ground Support
28 July	"	9:45		Merseburg
4 August	"	7:15		Hamburg
9 August	"	7:00		Furth
11 August	"	8:30		Belfort
35 Missions		267:15 Hours	4:00 Hours	

Record of thirty-five successful missions over enemy territory in the
lucky *The Mississippi Miss.*

- Courtesy of Colonel Howard T. Richardson (USAF Ret)

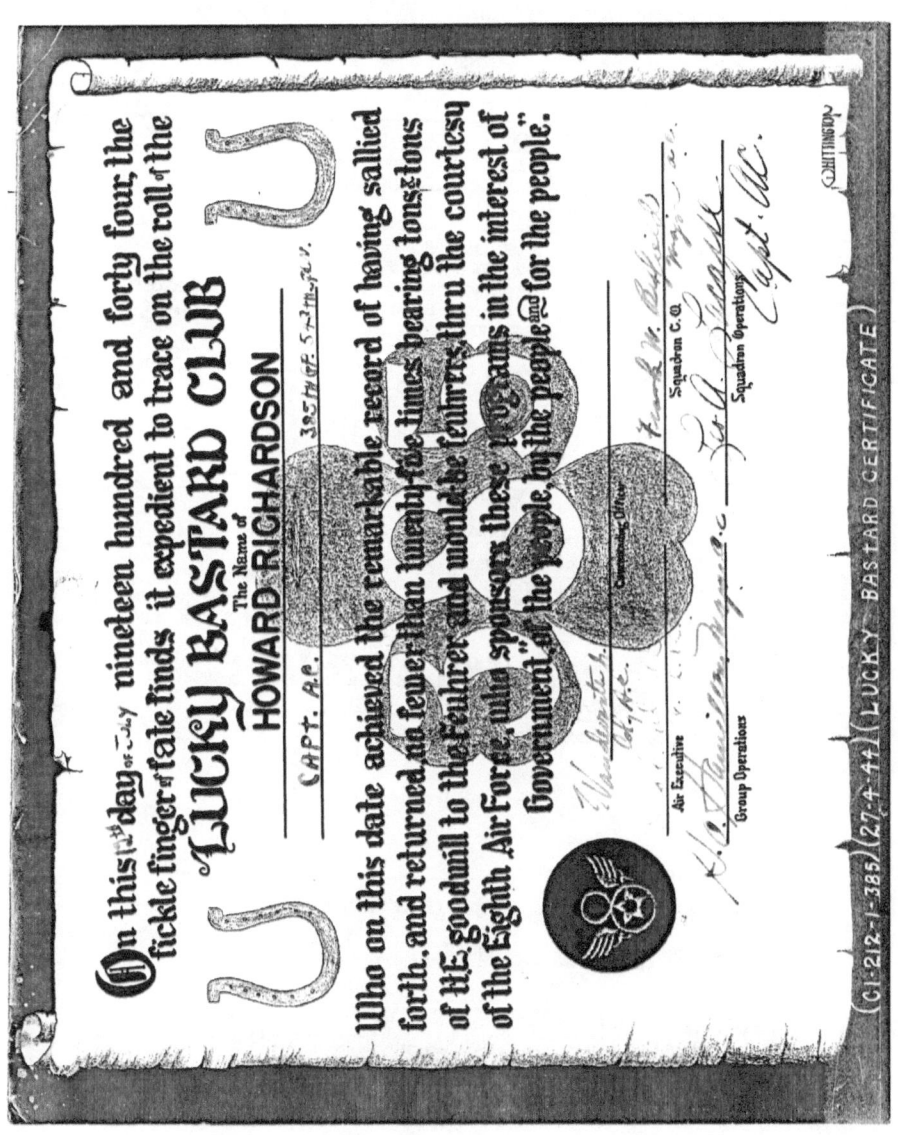

- Courtesy of Colonel Howard T. Richardson (USAF Ret)

CHARLES D. RICHARDSON

Form AL-569
Rev.(8-57)

U. S. Atomic Energy Commission
ALBUQUERQUE OPERATIONS

TEMPORARY CUSTODIAN RECEIPT (for maneuvers)

FROM: JAMES W. TWITTY COL USAF   DAECMR

DATE: 4 FEB 58

CERTIFICATE NUMBER: 2-044

NOUN	SERIAL NUMBER	MK	MOD	REMARKS (INCLUDE ASSOCIATED MAJOR ASSEMBLIES)
B	47782	15	Q	P.S 1500
C	Simulated	150		

(TEMPORARY CUSTODY IS BASED ON B SERIAL NUMBER LISTED ABOVE. MAJOR ASSEMBLIES COMPRISING THE WEAPON ARE ITEMIZED FOR RECORD PURPOSES ONLY.)

"I UNDERSTAND THAT, HAVING RECEIPTED FOR THE ABOVE ITEM(S) FROM THE ATOMIC ENERGY COMMISSION CUSTODIAN FOR THE SOLE PURPOSE OF FLYING IT ON A MANEUVER, IT WILL REMAIN IN THE CUSTODY OF THE ATOMIC ENERGY COMMISSION AND FOR THAT PURPOSE, AND DURING THIS MANEUVER, I SHALL ACT AS TEMPORARY CUSTODIAN FOR THE ATOMIC ENERGY COMMISSION. I WILL ALLOW NO ASSEMBLY OR DISASSEMBLY OF THIS ITEM(S) WHILE IN MY CUSTODY, NOR WILL I ALLOW ANY ACTIVE CAPSULE TO BE INSERTED INTO IT AT ANY TIME. I WILL, UPON RETURN FROM THIS MANEUVER, DELIVER THIS ITEM(S) UPON PROPER RECEIPT TO, AND ONLY TO, THE PROPERLY DESIGNATED ATOMIC ENERGY COMMISSION CUSTODIAN OR DESIGNATED AEC MILITARY REPRESENTATIVE.

349
A/C NUMBER   TEMPORARY CUSTODIAN   RANK   ORGANIZATION   30th Bomber

SPECIAL INSTRUCTIONS FOR TEMPORARY CUSTODIANS:
IN THE EVENT OF EMERGENCY OR UNSCHEDULED LANDINGS, AIRCRAFT MECHANICAL TROUBLE OF A SERIOUS AND DELAYING NATURE, OR IN ANY SITUATION CAUSING OR LIKELY TO CAUSE A BREAK IN AEC CUSTODY OF, MAJOR DAMAGE TO, OR LOSS OF THE MATERIAL, THE TEMPORARY CUSTODIAN WILL AT ONCE NOTIFY:
1. THE SHIPPER OF THE MATERIAL AS NAMED IN THE "FROM" LINE ABOVE, AND
2. SAC OR NAVY HEADQUARTERS, AS APPROPRIATE, FOR IMMEDIATE TRANSMITTAL TO USAEC, ALBUQUERQUE OPERATIONS OFFICE.

------ Tear along this line for return receipt to Aircraft Commander ------

DATE:

I HEREBY ACKNOWLEDGE RECEIPT FROM _____, AIRCRAFT

COMMANDER ON A/C # _____, OF THE ITEMS LISTED ON TEMPORARY CUSTODIAN

CERTIFICATE NUMBER _____ DATED _____.

ALOO/AEC directed
use of this form in
instructions to DAECMR's
dtd 1 Nov 57.

92287   FINAL RECIPIENT FOR AEC

Enclosure #1

Copy of the Temporary Custodian Receipt transferring custody of the bomb from the U.S. Atomic Energy Commission to Major Howard Richardson.

- Courtesy of Colonel Howard T. Richardson (USAF Ret)

CHARLES D. RICHARDSON has a rich and varied background in aviation. His experience includes instructor pilot, air traffic controller, Washington Consulting Group aviation instructor, and Naval Liaison Officer at the Atlantic Fleet Weapons Training Facility, Roosevelt Roads Naval Air Station.

He has published two previous books and is a freelance writer for *IFR Magazine*. Charles is a prolific writer and currently has two books under construction. He resides in south Texas with his wife.

Visit the author's website at www.bookprintpublishing.com

Cover art by Barry Ross